# Unraveled Faith

Sharon B. Burgess

Author

# Unraveled Faith



Published by Sharon Burgess, P.O. Box 393092,
Snellville Georgia 30039



Printed in the United States of America

ISBN: 978-0-578-16576-9

# DEDICATION

To my father, Pastor Weston Burgess Jr.,

and my loving mother, the late Della S. Burgess.

Mom, I wish you were here to celebrate this book with me.

You would be so proud.

I also dedicate this book to my sisters, Valrie, Sandy,

Christal, Carita, and Barbara.

My love for all of you is endless.

Special thanks to my children, Weston and Cyril III.

You all are my world. Thank you for being by my side

and giving me your love.

# INTRODUCTION

Growing up in a small church was quite a sheltering experience for me. It wasn't until I moved to Atlanta that I actually had the opportunity to experience the "Mega Church" phenomenon. I have to admit it wasn't all bad. I learned more about God and myself than ever before in my church-going life. It was revealing and liberating all at the same time. I experienced messages by pastors who were able to illuminate scriptures and leave me wanting to know more. So, yes, I do understand how congregations can grow to such large capacities. What Christian wouldn't want to learn about God and all of His goodness?

Leaders of mega churches are normally granted a broad range of power. This power is often misused and abused by a misappropriation of funds, a desire to build an empire of personal wealth, and occasionally a tendency to engage in sexual or moral impropriety with unwitting and gullible parishioners. This twisted feeling of omnipotence has led many Christians to distrust the church and ultimately break away from it.

When we know that these behaviors exist in the church, we have to be bold enough to execute the power that God has given us and avoid falling prey to leaders who do not exemplify godly behavior. God gives us the power of discernment, and we ought to exercise it. Churchgoers often seek an "emotional fill-up" for the week, and that's okay; we need to hear words of spiritual encouragement.

I am writing this book for all the Desirees and Lilas who have had to rethink their spiritual foundation and purpose. Usually this awakening occurs when we have been hurt by others or disappointed by life's circumstances. I hope this book raises a conscience thought of why we attend church, are we seeking spiritual growth, and are we just following in a religious tradition?

# ACKNOWLEDGEMENTS

To my sister Sandy, whose generosity and drive for success inspired me to begin writing this book and to finish it successfully. You helped me overcome a multitude of fears by applying your faith into my own personal action plan. You are the proven visionary in the family, and you keep us going and striving for greatness. I can't wait until your movie, *Disposable Income,* hits the big screen.

To my editors, Mike and Ralph Valentino, you have truly amazed me. Thank you for your insight and patience. Needless to say, I am forever grateful that we met. I can't wait to start on a new project with you.

To True World Order Entertainment: You guys are so talented and creative, it's beyond belief. Thank you for lending your creativity to this book. Your imagination will certainly take you further than your dreams.

Carleen Brown, you have helped me to grow as a writer and as a person. You are a talented writer, editor, and television producer, and you are equally great at them all. You have a talent and gift from God that everyone in the media industry should be so privileged to have. You are also a sweet, loving spirit and a tremendous source of joy in my life. There are big things awaiting you. W alk faithfully toward your destiny…

To editors: Garlaine Luc, and Byron Rivers, it was a pleasure working with you both, your input has been invaluable.

To my best friend Aileen: Thanks for your encouragement and prayers. Every time I said that I was going to do something new you always encouraged me with your few words—"Go ahead"—and that's what I needed to hear. You know more about me than anyone, and you have always given me unconditional love.

Additionally, I would like to thank a few special people God put in my path for reasons I don't quite yet fully understand, but I trust His direction: Valerie Edwards, you really kept me on track and gave me the push I most needed. You started working with me just at the right time. It's almost as if you could read my mind. Thank you most for your honesty and candid guidance.

Ernest McWhite – you are one of a kind and will always hold a special place in my heart. You always believed in me and that speaks volumes. Your love and encouragement means the world to me.

# CHAPTER ONE

Lila tiptoed out of little Royal's room, closing her son's door softly, and letting out a sigh. She had a busy morning getting the children prepared for school. Each morning she performed the same routine, but today brought about a completely new challenge.

Her two-year-old, Royal, had experienced a restless night, and Lila was far more tired than usual. Of her two oldest children, Jackson, now six, was in the first grade, and Latoya was in kindergarten. That morning Jackson argued about his lunch, and Latoya could never find contentment with her hairdo. On top of that, Lila had been running from one chore to the next, making sure the children had what they needed before the bus came. It all created a maddening explosion of childhood adrenaline working against parental fatigue.

Jackson was Lila and Lamont's love child, conceived long before they were married. That alone became a huge topic of gossip in their small town. After all, she *was* the preacher's daughter. With his dark chocolate skin and long legs, Jackson was the spitting image of Lamont.

Latoya, having a perfect mixture of Lila and Lamont's good looks, was no doubt her father's prized possession. With her long black hair, one could almost mistake her for a tall black Barbie doll. She constantly talked about her dad and swore he could do no wrong despite his absence. Latoya was wise beyond her years. Whenever something was bothering Lila, Latoya was the first to notice, always providing some consolation with a sensitive hug.

Though only twenty-six, Lila felt worn out from being mother, father, and sole provider for the family, even though her outward appearance gave no indication of the inner turmoil she experienced. She knew her smooth caramel skin and natural elegance far exceeded her circumstances, but it took the kids going off to school to offer a clue of what her possibilities could be.

*Thank God for enlightenment*, she thought. She knew that her inner strength from God kept her from losing her mind in the midst of her daily turmoil. The past few months had found her skipping church far too often. Although she felt convicted, she just couldn't muster the strength to hear the word from God as if it was the first time, when she already knew it too well.

She quietly went about her routine of fixing a cup of coffee and catching an episode of her favorite soap. Although way behind the story line, she didn't blame herself since it had been a hectic week.

The apartment was neat and clean, but the furnishings had now grown threadbare. Everything piqued with nostalgia as her eyes panned the room. From the small crack in the hallway mirror and the chip on the coffee table to the tiny holes in the walls, everything took on its own special meaning. They, like her, were all soldiers on that battlefield that became her marriage once Lamont began using drugs.

She and Lamont had only been divorced for two years, but she didn't like to linger on the wedding photo nestled beside the honeymoon pictures that led to more bad memories than the whole union deserved. She often thought of taking them down, but for the sake of reassuring the kids that they had a daddy and a family, she didn't. Sometimes they helped her, though, for they depicted a happier and simpler time.

Even their honeymoon at the cabin in the Smoky Mountains of Tennessee was simple because it lacked all pretense and glamour. That time with Lamont, alone and away from school and work —in a world before the unraveling took place—all felt so pure and so right. She loved everything about their honeymoon, from the twittering of the birds in the cool mountain mornings to the rugged pastoral setting. The gurgling of the brook that ran nearby to the everyday pleasure of the sometimes foggy, sometimes mystical mountains. The innocent rapture of being so close to the one she loved.

Those early days had been the most powerfully satisfying of her young life, and she was initially reluctant to forget them despite friends' urging. At times, though, those short trips down memory lane filled her with a longing so bitter yet so sweet that she could hardly bear it.

The sound of the steaming kettle aroused Lila from her trance. She quickly poured its contents into her favorite mug, set her old battered kettle on the stove, and walked gingerly into the living room. Turning on the TV, she settled her tall, attractive frame onto the couch. She tucked one long leg under the opposite thigh before wiggling to make herself comfortable while the lilting organ theme music of the soaps faded to the first scene. Just then, she jumped at a soft tap on the door.

Upon opening it, she discovered it was Desiree, the best friend she'd found since she had moved to Georgia. Lila instantly put her finger to her lips upon seeing her, but she wasn't hesitant. Desiree stepped inside wearing a big grin while tottering on stiletto heels with an exaggerated tiptoe. She whispered, "I didn't wanna take no chance on ringing the bell. You got me trained, girl."

Desiree was a flamboyant young woman whose aura exuded confidence. The twenty-five-year-old had a darker complexion than Lila's and she wielded hazel brown eyes, which she adorned with long false eyelashes. Ironically they were her most notable feature since they brought her the most compliments. Combined with her wit and charm, she not only commanded attention from men, but she usually got her way with them. A large diamond stud in the side of her nose sparkled with the hint that luxury had now become habit.

When both were settled on the couch with coffee, Desiree's eyes rolled over on her friend. "Girl, you looking fine," she said. "I see you're wearing makeup, and I know it's not to impress me." With a suspicious expression, she added, "What's up?"

"What's up with what? What are you saying?" Lila said, as innocently as she could.

"You look especially pretty today. That's what I'm saying. So, stop BS-ing me, girlfriend. What's hap'ning?"

"Nothing. Don't be silly," she replied.

"Look, Lila. How long we been hanging together now? Like I don't know you. I..."

Maybe it was the way Lila smiled and tossed her head or the way she flipped her soft shoulder-length hair around that gave Desiree the clue. She grinned. "Wait! I got it. Lamont's coming around today?"

Demurring a bit, Lila dropped her head and murmured, "He said he was. He promised to give me some money."

Desiree cocked her head at her friend with a sardonic

expression. If cynicism were an art, Desiree would be the Mona Lisa.

"I hope you ain't going to let him charm you," she said while rolling her eyes. "You know Lamont got that *thang* going on. Ain't never seen one of those basketball jocks who wasn't a ladies' man and a big-time player. They all prima donnas—all of them. The girls go loopy over them. Fall all over them. How can any man—weak creatures that they are—resist? I'll tell you how. They can't, and they don't! None of 'em. And that Lamont—he's the biggest prima donna of them all. And he can be as slippery as an eel, especially when he spreading that charm around. In fact, if he bottled that stuff, he could be rich. He don't like to work anyhow, you know."

The sadness lingered in the droop of Lila's shoulders and the distant look in her eyes. "C'mon, Desiree, you know how I feel about things. I know Lamont. I know all about him. He can barely take care of himself, let alone support a family. I know I'm making excuses for him, but I know if he comes up with any money at all, it was a tough thing for him to do. And for him, it's a big thing."

"Girl, you like a lot of sistahs I know; you too ready to let him off the hook. Lamont never been nothing but a player and a druggie. It's you who expects him to be something else."

"That's not true, Desiree. He is who he is. He was different before the drugs got him. And as far as him being a ladies' man, that was before he and I were married. We were so happy at first."

Lila went quiet. She knew she was getting defensive but couldn't help it. "He gives what he can. But you know his habit has ruined him. He's always one step out of rehab."

The girls took a sip of coffee, but Lila needed to talk. She kept on. "Before Lamont's injury, we had a very promising future. When he couldn't play basketball any longer, he turned to using drugs. I guess it somehow eased his pain."

"Well, he sure has left *you* in a lot of pain."

"I just told him: 'Don't you ever, ever put me in the projects.' While I got a breath of life left in me, I am not going to put us in the projects, even if he is gone and I don't have much money. I won't have my kids growing up in that foul atmosphere."

Desiree had lapsed into silence, and Lila noticed. It was odd for her usually exuberant friend. Lila said, "What's the matter? Did I say something?"

Desiree, now uncharacteristically distant, stirred her coffee. "I never told you I come out of the projects down in Mobile?" She leveled what was for her a rather serious gaze at Lila. "You know I'm no Atlanta girl. You know about Mobile."

"Of course, I—I just didn't know about the projects."

Now it was Lila who turned silent. When she did speak, it was halting. "I'm sorry, Desiree. I didn't mean anything by it. I just know what happens to people who…"

Desiree stretched out a hand with long tapered fingernails and touched her friend's arm. "No need to go on, girl. I know. Believe me, I know. My kid sister got three kids, and she knocked up again. She's not even nineteen yet. My brother, he's still in jail. You don't need to tell me."

Just as quickly as she went down, Desiree rose on an enthusiastic wave. "Shoot, girl, if I wanted to be down, I would have gone to visit my kin. Now," she said, reaching into her oversized leather handbag. "Let me sweeten up that coffee for you."

"No," Lila protested. "C'mon, Desiree, you know I don't drink."

"Yeah, and that's a problem we got to work on. Lighten up. I know what they tell you down at that …What is it? True God church you go to…"

Lila interrupted and said, "True Faith Christian Church. And they don't preach total abstinence. They just say not to abuse alcohol. I don't drink. I don't have a taste for it."

Desiree raised her arched brows even further. "Taste for it? How can you get a taste for it? You've never had a drink."

Lila thought she heard the baby stir, so she got up and tiptoed into the room.

She emerged from little Royal's room to catch Desiree putting a bottle into her knockoff Gucci purse. Lila smiled at Desiree and said, "Girl is that what I think it is? It is too early in the morning for you to be sipping."

---

Avoiding Lila's comments, Desiree asked, "How is little Royal?"

"He's teething and hardly slept at all last night. I stayed up half the night rubbing his gums with ice chips and reading him bedtime stories."

"You used ice chips?"

"Yeah, it's an old remedy I heard my mother talk about. Besides, I don't like giving him all that pain medication. It's just not good to have all that stuff in his little system."

Desiree smiled. "You're a good mama, Lila."

As Lila took a sip of coffee, her friend averted her eyes. At first, Lila said nothing and took another sip. Then she said, "Desiree, you are evil. I said I didn't want any alcohol."

"Oh, come on. Loosen up. You got a world of grief for a life. You gotta learn to loosen up or you gonna flip out on me."

"I'm doing okay," Lila said with little sincerity.

"Yeah, you're great. Three kids and a druggie husband who leaves you to fend for your own self. How you ever gonna find you another man in this situation? I'll tell you how…"

Desiree was off on one of her rants. "You ain't—that's how! You gotta have yourself some fun while you still young, kiddo.

You can't just work, work, work and forget that there's a world of fun and people out there. And you're a looker; you won't have no trouble at all out there."

Lila intentionally took another sip of the spiked coffee. She was used to her friend's repartee, and though she resisted, she appreciated that Desiree did indeed care about her. And Lila's response was part of the repartee.

"Desiree, the trouble with you is that you think there is no life after men. Men aren't the answer to everything."

"Maybe not, girl, but I don't go around thinking I'm going to find me a Prince Charming. I just have fun with the dudes. If they can have fun with women and go from lady to lady, I can have fun with men and tomorrow…" She snapped her fingers. "Poof! I be done with them, just like they was gonna do me. You see, like them, I too know how to play the game. Even the married ones want to play."

Lila wanted to correct Desiree, but she knew this was a sore subject. Her friend's mood remained aggressive. "Shoot, the married ones, they the worst. But I let them know I don't want them; I only want to borrow them. When they think they are playing me, I'm really playing them."

While taking another sip of coffee, Lila thought about her friend's remarks. She remembered how men had hurt Desiree most of her life. From her father, who had left her, to the men who had made broken promises, she'd felt enough hurt and pain to power a steamboat. Lila knew at this time that it was better to let her vent. She leaned over and nudged Desiree's arm.

"You are so cynical. I'm sorry life has beaten down on you like that."

"That's why I work at being up."

"You sure do that." Lila smirked sarcastically, taking another sip of her spiked coffee, unknowingly getting a buzz.

Desiree lost her upbeat mood, despite the vodka. An unfamiliar and uncharacteristic quiet descended like a rain cloud over her.

"What's the matter, babe?" Lila inquired.

"Nothing."

Lila let it go, feeling uncomfortable about pushing her. That's when the next vodka bottle appeared. Lila decided not to protest when Desiree refreshed her drink, which was more like hot vodka than coffee laced with vodka.

Lila waited patiently, knowing that her friend couldn't, nor wouldn't, remain quiet for long. She was ready when she finally did speak up.

"I never told you everything about Mobile. Did I?"

"You told me about school, but I didn't know about the projects till just now. But—"

Desiree cut her off. "I never told you about my baby."

Lila's jaw dropped at her friend's unexpected admission. Desiree was always up front and personal with everything. So, it was almost impossible to believe that she had kept something like this under wraps for so long.

"What? You had a baby?"

"Yep, I sure did."

Lila waited, too polite to interrupt or to pressure her for more details, even though that was her impulse.

---

Desiree said, "I was only sixteen. I had no job."

"And his father?"

"His daddy was in jail."

"So?"

Desiree dropped her head. "I went to the adoption place."

"You…?"

"Yeah, that's what I done."

Another awkward silence more than a dozen heartbeats long followed as Lila struggled to wrap her mind around the thought that Desiree held such a secret. Lila felt that it was her place to wait rather than prompt for more.

As tears welled up in Desiree's eyes, she confessed, "I had no way to raise him. Oh, did I say it was a boy?"

Lila shook her head in disbelief and with sincere compassion in her heart.

Desiree was distant when she talked and more distant than Lila had ever seen her. "Yeah, he was a handsome little rascal. Had hazel and brown eyes like me…and the cutest little cupid mouth. Like a little angel he was. I thought I would die when they came and took him away. Till this day, I still have this ole ache in my heart."

"I'm sorry, Des. I know how that must hurt."

In the two-and-a-half years that Lila had known Desiree, she had never once seen her cry. Lila wrapped her arms around her and let her sob into her shoulder.

"I'm sorry to go on blubbering like that," she said. It's so not me." Desiree was a master at hiding her true feelings. She had built up walls to protect her heart, not knowing that one day she would have to face all her fears.

"I know," Lila replied with a tone of compassion, as only a woman who had given birth to a child could offer. She held Des's hand gently. "It's okay. That's what friends are for."

When she was composed enough to speak, Desiree said, "That's why I look at you sometimes—with your three beautiful kids, all alone, bringing 'em up by yourself—and feel most ashamed. Maybe I could have done it too. But I didn't think, at least back then, that I ever could do it. I had no confidence in myself then."

---

It was a bit of a shock to see this vulnerability exposed in a person Lila had always considered strong and capable, although her past haunted her like an ever-present shadow. Pondering to find the right words, she finally exclaimed, "Well, you certainly do now."

"You think so?" she said with a final sniffle.

"Of course I do. I don't know anybody with as much confidence as you."

Lila was touched and concerned at the same time, now realizing that people are not always exactly what they appear to be. Desiree was hiding some real pain. She was so outgoing and so bubbly—who would ever think it? But there it was, laid out for her to see—a vulnerability that told her what kind of girl she really was.

Lila sipped her coffee, apparently deep in thought. She was getting ready to offer Des a proposal. Finally, she said, "Why don't you come to church with me on Sunday?"

Desiree rolled her eyes. "Girl, I know I been weepy and seem like a basket case, but don't go trying to make no Holy Roller out of me!"

"I'm not, Desiree. It's just that the Lord is what we all need.

Not just me. Not just you. Everybody needs the Lord. Go to God. He'll lighten your burden. He'll help you feel worthy, like you're important."

Desiree cocked her head and gazed at her friend. "Do I seem like I don't feel important to you? I just told you how I run these foolish men around and make them pant after me like a pack of wolves. Does that seem like I got low self-esteem?"

"Maybe I didn't say it right. I mean that God is the best support you're ever gonna get in this life. I know that for sure. If it wasn't for His love, I don't know where I'd be right now. Probably have lost my kids and be in some women's shelter."

Desiree said, "I doubt that. I—"

Just then, her cell phone chimed in with a rock beat. She got on the phone, and Lila stood up to put the coffee cups in the sink. When she returned, Desiree was putting the phone back in her Gucci bag and standing up with a devilish smirk.

With some disappointment in her voice, Lila said, "You going already?"

"Gotta go, girl. Give that little angel, little Royal, a hug and a kiss from his Auntie Desiree. Oh, yes, and kiss Jackson and Latoya for me too."

Lila responded, "Okay, I will," feeling rather sad to see her friend leave.

Desiree headed for the door with a resilient pep in her step. And with a final over-her-shoulder warning, she said, "Now don't let that Lamont sweet-talk you. You be wary of that man. He done you enough wrong already as it is. I'll call you tonight."

# CHAPTER TWO

On her way to answer the door, Lila paused in the hallway mirror to tuck an errant wisp of hair back and look herself over. For a brief moment, she reminisced about better times with Lamont—when trying to look her best for him felt exciting. She snapped back to reality after opening the door and seeing Lamont standing there as she knew him.

His appearance was what she'd come to expect these days. More often than not, he looked strung out, with dark circles under his eyes. For a fastidious person, he was fairly disheveled, like a man who didn't expect much of anything, least of all himself. His masculine physique had diminished, and he was gaunt and emaciated. However, she never knew what to expect of his mood. It depended on how strung out he was or if he was coming off a high and needed another fix. Usually, he was still able to maintain some of his old jauntiness.

Lila remembered so well when Lamont started using drugs. It

was after he injured his ankle very badly one night in a college basketball game. He was a legitimate star player and received the best star treatment, but the promise of physical therapy fell short, and he never regained his speed. After his coach reduced his minutes, he was relegated to the bench.

As more time passed, he ultimately was cut from the team. Shortly after that, he started smoking pot occasionally. Everybody felt that pot was no big deal. He even tried to get Lila to take a few hits with him, especially before making love, but she resisted. The very idea was abhorrent, yet he persisted.

She thought she was immune to his prodding until one night she gave in. She had a feeling that if she didn't, they wouldn't make love that night. This led to an epiphany, revealing that lovemaking was the only bond they had left and therefore the only glue remaining that joined them together to any degree, for what that was worth.

When he coached her on how to hold the joint and inhale, she wound up choking and gagging. "What foul stuff!" she cried. Handing it back to him compelled her to ask, "How can you stand it?"

"It takes some getting used to," he advised as though it were a finely aged wine that only a cultured person could understand.

It seemed like yesterday when hope had ruled the day. The Atlanta Hawks were scouting him and he'd always looked his best while excelling in school. However, after the injury, Lamont lost hope. That's when he started dabbling with cocaine. From there he became hooked on crack. That sealed his fate because things went downhill fast from there. He couldn't keep his grades up and lost his scholarship before dropping out of school altogether.

As usual, when she saw what he had done to himself, her heart sank to new depths. Once an intelligent, vibrant young man, he now lived as though he had lost every care in the world. Old memories could no longer hold their own when competing with the ugliness of the present.

Unfortunately, that included the ripe fruit of Lila and the kids—fruit left on the tree, which was meant for a family pie that never made it to the oven.

She saw his darting eyes and had an idea what shape he was in.

She invited him in and whispered, “Royal is sleeping.”

Their meetings of late were usually awkward and stressful, and judging from his overactive pupils, this one was going to be bad. He plopped aimlessly down on the couch. She sat opposite him and crossed her ankles. “About the money…” he started.

A long sigh hissed through her lips. She knew what was coming. “Lamont, I’m out of baby food, and my check doesn’t come for three more days. What am I supposed to do?”

Lamont slapped his forehead with his palm and muttered, “I don’t know what to do.” He sat up and dropped his head into his hands, and she resisted her usual sympathy for him.

When he raised his head, he said, “Truth is, I was hoping you could lend me a few bucks till I get some money.”

She clenched her fists. “I have no money, Lamont. Just what I get from the state and that goes too fast. I have three kids to take care of.”

He muttered, “I don’t know what to do.” Before she could answer, he said, “Can’t you borrow from your girlfriend—what’s-her-name…?”

"Desiree."

"Yeah, or from your dad."

"I'm all borrowed out. Aunt Nona and Dad help me all they can, which also includes babysitting. I won't ask Desiree, either. I'm not going to borrow any more money, especially when I know I have no way of paying it back. After all, I have some pride."

"Just for a short while," he intoned, his voice pleading. "I don't know what to do."

She shook her head. "What to do? The answer's simple. You get off drugs and get a job; that's how a man supports his family. There are clinics to help you kick the habit. People do it all the time. How is it more difficult for you?"

Lamont raised his head, made eye contact, and stared at her. "Like I don't know that? What do you think I am? Some kind of lowlife? Some kind of fool?"

With a soft voice, Lila replied, "I don't know what you are these days. You tell me."

His pride now undoubtedly hurt, he then leaped to his feet and stormed out with tears welling in the corners of his eyes.

The next morning Lila ushered the two older kids off to school and then commenced preparations for her job interview. The job was a part-time position in the bookstore at the True Faith Christian Church. She had a personal interview with the pastor, Bishop Hines.

It had been almost two years since she'd been laid off from her job at the local drugstore where she was the floor manager. This interview was a big deal to Lila. She was tired of getting public assistance for herself, and she and the kids wanted much more out of life. This job held the hope of a new start.

Marcie, her next-door neighbor's daughter, would watch the kids whenever she had errands to run. Although Marcie was only eighteen, she was very responsible. She was taking night classes to become a schoolteacher, and the kids loved her. But she was not available this time to help out, so her Aunt Nona was the next sure thing.

Aunt Nona, a slim woman Lila adored, was on time. She looked at least ten years younger than her age and had a spunky attitude. Aunt Nona had always been there for Lila and the kids since Lila's mother died three years earlier. Lila felt close to her Aunt Nona, with her petite frame. She even looked just like Lila's mother. To Lila, she was so much more than an aunt.

When she saw Lila all dressed up, her glamorous aunt put her hands on her hips and said, "Chile, you looking mighty good today." Her words almost mimicked what her mother would have said. This brought a nostalgic smile to Lila's face. "I'm saying a prayer for you getting that job."

"Thanks, Auntie. Royal's still down for his nap. I put a bottle in the fridge for when he wakes up."

"Girl, are you still letting him suck a bottle?"

"You know how he is. He'll be howlin' for it. Latoya and Jackson will be home soon from school. Please have them start their homework and don't let them watch TV."

She smiled and said, "Go on, Chile. I raised two of my own. I still remember the ropes. In fact, I'm going to get Royal off that bottle."

"Good luck," she said as she headed out the door.

Lila parked the old Toyota in the shade, which lately was a

blessing to find. The summer was hot, even for Georgia. She tended to hold her breath every time she started up the old car, thanking God when it started as if the Almighty shined his light down solely for that purpose.

Halfway to the church, the Toyota began to buck and Lila noticed the temperature gauge running high. *Darn!* she thought. *Didn't the man at the gas station say something to her about the radiator the last time she had the oil checked?* The kids had been fussing in the backseat, and Royal was screaming so loudly that she hardly heard the man.

The car continued to act up as she reached True Faith Christian Church, which was located on the corner of Lake and Peachtree. It was a modern brick building, with clean lines and a rather stately oaken cross on the lower part of the rising steeple. The steeple itself was majestic and soared high above the other buildings in the neighborhood. The lawn and shrubbery around the building and the parking lot were professionally manicured, and they set off the building like a jewel in a crown.

The sight of this temple of God, this house of the Lord, always stirred her heart. When she thought of the spiritual comfort available inside those walls, it always calmed her soul and gave her hope.

When Lila pulled into the parking lot of the church, a cloud of steam erupted from the hood. “Darn,” she mumbled to herself. She got out and stood back, staring at the cloud as the car continued to hiss with a gurgling sound.

She was so absorbed in the newest problem in her troubled life that the deep male voice approaching her from behind took her by surprise.

“Afternoon, sister. I see you’ve got car problems.”

She turned and had to crane her neck to look up at the tall, handsome man. It was Bishop Hines, and he now stood beside her. The bishop could be, depending on the observer, an intimidating character. The gray at his temples added to his distinguished appearance, but he had a rugged masculinity and super–cheerful demeanor that one doesn’t ordinarily associate with a man of God.

Her own father was also a minister. She had subliminally

thought of him as a typical representative of the Lord. He was traditional and much more stern and formal. Bishop Hines appeared to be a happy, pleasant man who seemed much like everyone else in outlook and speech.

"Oh, hello, Bishop," she said. "Yeah. I know they build Toyotas to last, but I don't think the Lord can spare this old wreck much longer."

"Cheer up, sister. These kinds of problems may distress us at the time, but there are always sure solutions. God doesn't put more on us than we can handle."

She dropped her eyes a bit, feeling somewhat guilty for her whining.

He said, "You go on in and take a seat in my office. I'll be right in. Tell Sister Linda that I would like her to bring us in a couple of cold lemonades."

"Okay, Bishop. But please be careful. The car looks very hot."

"Not to worry, sister. I've spent some time under car hoods in my day." He beckoned for the security guard, who used to work as a mechanic before he got the job at the church.

The bishop's office was air-conditioned, and the cool air raised her spirits. By the time the bishop returned, his secretary had served them lemonade and cookies, and Lila was feeling a little better. Ever since she had been a little girl at her father's church, Mount Carmel, being in the house of the Lord always made her feel better no matter what was going on in her life.

Bishop Hines said, "Excuse me, sister," as he went into the bathroom adjacent to his office to wash his hands. When he returned, he said, "James and I think there's a leak in your radiator. We put in some sealant and water. We think that should hold it together until you can get it repaired."

"Thank you so much, Bishop. I hate to be such a bother. Lamont used to take care of the car. I know nothing more than to put gas in it and ask the man to check the oil every once in a while."

"No problem, sister. Now, about the job in the church bookstore…I understand from Sister Belinda that you are interested."

"Well, yeah, I am. The hours are great, but I do have a problem."

"What's that?"

She had trouble having a conversation with this man. He was so handsome that it was hard to look at him without admiring him and even fantasizing a little. She felt like a schoolgirl, becoming all flustered in his presence.

He had to ask again, "The problem, Lila? What is your problem?"

"Oh, yeah, it's my son Royal. The other two kids are in school, but I have to arrange for a babysitter for him. My aunt works and isn't available all the time."

The bishop said, "I see," and began rummaging through one of the many manila folders on his desk.

A minute later he said, "I'm looking to see what progress we have made in Sister Rosalind's plans to run a day-care center for our parishioners. It will be based on what you can afford. And I see here that we are almost ready to open. One more inspection by the state board on child care and we will be ready. So, you can bring the baby here for child care and pick him up at the end of your shift, getting you home in time for the other kids."

"Oh, that would be great," Lila said, unable to keep the gushing out of her voice. "How much would it cost? I have to figure it against what I'll make at the bookstore."

Bishop Hines folded his hands and leaned forward to take full interest in the young woman and her needs. "We haven't ironed out all the details about the day-care center yet. We will cross that bridge when the day care opens. For now, just meet with Deacon Pierce. He is the manager of the bookstore, and he will work out the details of your schedule and make it work for you."

Lila brightened. "Oh, thank you," she said. "That will be great." She wanted to leap across the desk and hug him but she resisted. He must have seen her enthusiasm, for he reached across the desk for her hands, which he held tenderly for a moment before releasing her.

"Your car should have cooled down by now, and you should be able to drive it home. I sure hope you can get it fixed for your new job which, incidentally," he said, looking at his calendar, "will start next Monday."

"I'll have to ask Lamont to look at the car for me. We can't afford a mechanic."

"How is Lamont? Is he still struggling with his problem?"

Lowering her eyes, she said, "Yes. He's worse than ever, I'm afraid."

Bishop Hines shook his head. "I hate to see what's happened to that man. If he was from the streets, maybe you could understand it a little better. I know the injury and not playing basketball was hard for him, but to throw his future away on drugs seems like more than the usual waste of human life. Unlike most of the kids in the streets, Lamont should have known better. He's an educated man and an intelligent man. He had benefits some of his contemporaries did not. I remember him as one fine basketball player too. I think I was pretty good in my day, but Lamont was even better. He has natural grace and talent. It's a shame to see him selling himself short."

As Bishop Hines continued with his thoughts of Lamont's downfall, he began to sound as if he were preaching a sermon.

Holding up his hands with excitement, he exclaimed, "Well, that's why I always teach my congregation: 'But seek ye first the kingdom of God, and all his righteousness, and these things shall be added unto you.' Yes, that's what the good book says, and we must put on the whole armor of God to be able to fight the wiles of the devil."

Calming down, he pondered a moment and then added, "That boy was one of the best power forwards I have ever seen."

Lila didn't have a response. Coming from the bishop, a man of authority, the speech made her realize just what a tragedy Lamont's life had become. She thought he would offer some solution or even try reaching out to Lamont. Instead, he dwelled on Lamont's current situation. That didn't sit right with her, but she didn't want to dwell on it.

She was grateful. At least he helped her to get a job. Knowing she was employed now gave her a little uplift and forced her mind off the circumstance that was of Lamont. It was like someone lifting the barbell of responsibility that she carried every day.

"I agree, but at this stage, Bishop, he's pretty hopeless. He can't help me support the kids, and I don't want to go to the court with it because he'll only wind up in jail. I couldn't stand that. I just pray he comes to his senses and one day he has a productive life again…"

She stopped, feeling that she was about to choke up.

He reached over again and took her hands, holding them a little longer this time. "If you have a real problem with the car, let me know. We have funds from the benevolence offerings, and we use that money to help those who have given generously to the church and, in return, are now in need themselves. You may qualify for some of those funds."

Lila said, "No, thank you." She hadn't given very often because she had little to give, and she didn't want him looking into her financial contributions—or lack thereof. It was embarrassing enough that he had fixed her car.

"Thank you again, Bishop," she said, rising. "I've got to get home. The kids will be getting off the bus soon."

"Go with the Lord, sister."

"And you too, Bishop. Bye."

As she put the key into the Toyota's ignition, she said a little prayer. It started up, but she still worried until she got home.

Little Royal was up when she walked in. Her aunt, as usual, was spoiling him with treats, and to Lila's surprise, he was holding a sippy cup. She reached for him. "How's my little man?" she cooed. "What is this you have?" He was holding the cup by the handle, swinging it back and forth and calling out, "Mama."

"Auntie, this is a miracle." Lila and her Aunt Nona burst into laughter, knowing it would take more than just a few hours to wean Royal off the bottle.

"One day at a time and only a bottle at bedtime," she remarked to Lila as she was gathering her things to leave.

Lila loved this baby child. Although she did not favor one of her kids over the other, Royal was conceived when she and Lamont were at their lowest point. She knew in her heart that she shouldn't have had Royal. She knew that their prospects were not good, but she had hoped that this baby would help pull Lamont together and help him see the obligations he had to his growing family.

But, of course, it didn't. The evil of the drugs was far stronger than any paternal instincts he might have had. What the new baby *had* done, in fact, was drive him to desperation. He now had three kids to support and was unable to keep a job.

When her aunt left, she went to the refrigerator to get some cold water, and she spotted the groceries. The fridge was full. She knew that her aunt had brought them and left them out in the car until she had gone, knowing she would protest. She stared at the food, her eyes filled with tears.

Everyone was trying hard to help her, even Desiree, in her own way. After she left, there were times when Lila would find a twenty tucked under something on the coffee table. She knew it was useless to protest. Desiree wasn't the kind of person to listen to her protests. Funny that at times Lila wished that she were more like Desiree. And just this morning Desiree had confessed to her that she had wished she were more like Lila.

*The human condition*, she thought, *always wanting what someone else has—or at least we think we want it.*

She knew deep down that her personal salvation rested with

the Lord. Without Him, she wasn't going to be able to get through this. No amount of partying would get her through for sure.

# CHAPTER THREE

As usual, Deacon William Pierce, the manager of the True Faith Christian Church bookstore, arrived early to work. He had been dedicated to the church for five years but had already managed the bookstore for two. Bishop Hines held Deacon Pierce in the highest regard and trusted him immensely, at least far above all the other deacons who were arguably trustworthy. People who knew him called him Bill.

At thirty-six, Bill wielded the physique of a much younger man. He had silky black hair and appeared to be of Greek descent, though most folks usually guessed rather than ask. Although uniquely handsome, he was modest about his looks and the carnal attention it brought.

Bill was married to his high school sweetheart and was obsessed about the fact that they didn't have any children—a disappointment that weighed on his shoulders lately. Although he loved managing the church bookstore and was young enough to enjoy life, this void didn't allow him to do it fully.

However, Bill did find some solace. His job at the bookstore brought him a measure of satisfaction, and his ministerial assignment of mentoring flock who'd gone astray gave his life untold value when God gave him the wisdom to look in their eyes after doing so.

Bill was now preparing for a very busy Monday. He recalled the Sunday services of yesterday as he did and pondered how Bishop Hines had made a special push for more financial support. He had asked his flock to support the True Faith Christian Church and all its entities, including the children's fund, the choir fund, and especially the bookstore.

Bishop Hines was a charismatic speaker, and something unique about his aura made the congregation want to do whatever he asked twice at the mere mention of it. Bill didn't quite understand the necessity for more fund requests, though. After all, the bishop had never mentioned a lack of support during the financial meeting with the board of directors.

As Bill was going over publisher invoices due for payment that week, he looked up and noticed the bishop approaching. There was something about Bishop Hines. He was a physically large man and his swaggering gait usually found him storming into a room far more often than simply entering it. His stature alone could command your attention, and whether you knew him or not, his walk often made you wonder if it was happenstance or his design that made you take notice.

"Good morning, Bill."

Bill put his invoice aside and looked up. "Good morning, Bishop."

Bishop Hines flashed him one of his biggest, broadest smiles. "How are you with the Lord this morning?"

"Fine, Bishop, fine. But I have a feeling that we are all more satisfied with ourselves than the Lord is with us."

The bishop smiled his wide, disarming smile. "True, Deacon; so true."

Bill had a feeling that there was something more to the bishop's visit than the cheery greeting.

The bishop's eyes roamed the store, and he appeared to be

taking account of the shelves stocked with bibles, devotionals, and journals. A life-size poster of him stood next to the register where CDs and DVDs of his sermons were neatly stacked on the shelf. Next to that was a bare shelf.

"Are we so fortunate that my book sold out this last weekend and that's why none are on display this morning?"

"That's true, Bishop," Bill responded. "Sales are going very well."

Hines leaned into the young man in a confidential manner and said, "Bill, please be sure to have my book on display at all times. Keep some copies under the counter in case the Lord continues to bless us with high sales."

Bill lapsed from his morose demeanor to one of earnest. "Oh, sure, Bishop. I just haven't gotten to it yet this morning."

"I understand, Bill." The bishop started to move away but stopped and turned. Somehow, this gesture made Bill tense up. "Oh, and I hope you haven't forgotten to exclude my book sales from the others and render all receipts and publisher invoices to me."

"I haven't forgotten."

Hines smiled again and was off.

Bill stopped arranging invoices and hurried to restock the bishop's book, *In the Name of Jesus,* on its prominent perch on top of and above all the others—and in the front of the store. He did wonder about the bishop's personal financial agreement with the publisher, but he had too much to do to concern himself about it for too long.

Bill was just ringing up a sale when Bishop Hines returned. He waited patiently until the elderly customer was ready to leave, but before she did, the old woman turned around and spotted the bishop. It was now an event, and the woman paused and broke into a huge smile.

"Why, good morning, Bishop."

"Good morning, Sister Clara. How goes things with you and the Lord?"

"Fine, Bishop; just fine. She kind of glanced down at the book in her hand and said, "I can't wait to read your book. I've heard so much about it."

"Well, thank you, Sister. I only pray that with my humble words and the Lord's guidance, you'll get some inspiration from it."

"I'm sure I will, Bishop. Again, good morning to you."

"Good day, dear Sister."

Bishop Hines then turned to Bill. "Bill, I forgot to mention that I'm sending over a candidate for the part-time book clerk job. Her name is Lila Thompson."

Bill waited expectantly. He was getting used to the bishop in the five years he had been at True Faith Christian, and he knew he would have something else to say.

Hines said, "Now, as you know, I don't interfere with your job of managing the bookstore. I leave it in your competent hands. But I know from personal references that this young lady is a fine person and an upstanding member of the church. I hope you will give her…not preferential consideration, of course, but adequate consideration. She has three small kids too, you know, so you might have to work around her schedule. Just…just please be sure to give her every consideration, alright?"

"Of course, I will."

"Thanks again, Bill. I'll see you at the Monday night meeting?"

"As usual, Bishop."

As the imposing man left, Bill thought about his comment. He knew that the bishop was actually *telling* him to hire this Lila Thompson. While this type of pressure went against his grain, Bill knew that he was fully expected to do it. She probably was everything that the bishop said. However, the young man knew that Bishop Hines truly ran everything, which meant that any pretense of autonomy in running the bookstore was more imagination than reality.

On the other hand, everything else was quite satisfactory, and while Bill didn't have the final say on everything, he did have a measure of control over the bookstore operation.

Either way the bookstore's operation wasn't his life dream—at least not these days. He and his wife, Renee, had been married for ten years now, and nothing outweighed the self-induced funk they'd found themselves in over their inability to conceive a child.

In the sunny days of their courtship and early marriage, they never dreamed of such a problem, but now he prayed every day that the Lord would bless them with a child. They'd done their part for sure. He and Renee had taken all the tests. Even he—the modest, humble man that he was—had undergone the rather embarrassing sterility test that proved he, in fact, could have children.

But, so far, the Lord had not seen fit to bless them with this gift, despite the fact that they prayed daily seeking His favor. Bill and Renee were among the few non–African Americans in the True Faith congregation. They had been seeking a new church and, like wandering pilgrims, were invited to a sermon. They had immediately fallen in step with the rest, having been mesmerized by Bishop Hines, and were devoted to following him.

It was break time and Bill had time to sip coffee and daydream a bit. He was thinking of life's ironies—how so many of the families he had counseled over the years had just the opposite problem. The Lord had given them more children than they could handle or afford. Some were bad, and some were good, but at least these folks were blessed with children to begin with. Have mercy!

Without question, he had never counseled anybody with the problem he and his wife had. He knew he had married Renee because he loved her for better or worse, but now questioned whether they had grown apart. Perhaps the toll of not being able to have children had somehow caused their love to fade, but he tried to dismiss this possibility.

He was still far away when he heard a voice say rather loudly, "Mr. Pierce?"

"What?" Bill was embarrassed by his meandering. He looked up to see an attractive young woman standing before the counter.

Pointing to his name tag, she said, "You are Mr. Pierce…the manager, aren't you?"

Lila had recognized him from church services, but she had never formally met him. Getting red in the face, he said, "I'm sorry. I guess I was off somewhere. It's been a busy morning."

"I understand. I'm Lila Thompson. Bishop Hines told me he had set up an appointment for me."

"Yes, he told me about you." Bill called for one of his clerks to take over the cash register and then turned back to face Lila. "Come on into the office."

In the office, Bill sat at his desk as Lila handed over her resume.

As his eyes reviewed the resume, he hoped it wasn't obvious that he wasn't reading the words. Lila Thompson's beauty had caught him by surprise.

*I would remember her from church services had I seen her before,* he thought. There was definitely something about Lila that sparked Bill's interest for sure.

He didn't see any point in beating around the bush, especially since the bishop had told him she was his choice, so he offered, "The job is yours, Lila. Now, Bishop Hines said that you might have some scheduling problems?"

Her eyes widened.

"You mean I have the job?"

"Yes. Now, what is your schedule?"

Lila now appeared to be the one who was flustered. "I have a babysitter in the morning for my youngest, but I have to be home for the other two by two thirty."

Bill took a clipboard down from the wall behind him and scanned it. "Okay, how does nine to two on Monday, Wednesday, and Thursday sound?"

Beaming, Lila said, "It sounds great, Mr. Pierce."

"Good. Then can we expect you next Monday at nine?"

"Of course," she said, standing. "And thank you, Mr. Pierce."

"Call me Bill."

"Sure. Thank you, Bill. See you at nine on Monday."

Bill sat across from Bishop Hine's desk for their usual Monday afternoon business meeting. The office wasn't plush. It was tasteful but not overstated. The furniture was new, stylish, and eclectic—but not in any way ostentatious.

Pictures of the bishop during the high points of his ministry adorned the walls. There were photos of him with the mayor, with Jesse Jackson, and with other church officials. The one occupying a commanding place on the wall right behind his desk depicted him shaking hands with the famed evangelist Billy Graham.

The bishop had sent for coffee and his secretary served it on a silver tea set. Bill was thoughtfully stirring in sugar when the bishop, with his usual intuition, asked him, “Any problems to address, Bill?”

After a few sips, Bill did present him with a problem. “Bishop, with regard to the quarterly profit-and-loss statement for the bookstore, I don’t know how to enter the sales or payouts for your book. How do you want me to handle it?”

The bishop leaned forward and placed his elbows on his desk. He formed a steeple with his fingers and rested his chin at the peak. “Well, I, uh…I’m using the proceeds for a favorite charity of mine, and I want to keep everything separate from the bookstore.”

Bill sat waiting patiently for more.

“Let me see…” said Bishop Hines, who seemed lost in thought for a minute or two. “Do you have any ideas about how we can handle this, Bill?”

“Well,” Bill replied, “there’s money that has been put aside, as you asked. It isn’t in any of the deposits for the quarters. You told me you were handling the payouts to the publisher, so I imagine you will need the sales receipts to make the invoice payments.

How you want to handle the profits is up to you, I guess."

Hines thought some more. "Can we list a lot of them as returns?"

"Well, you still have to pay the publisher. If a book hasn't been returned, we don't have the return confirmation for it."

"But we can list them as returned."

"Yes, but again, how are you…?"

"Let me worry about that. So, the answer for you is to turn over the cash to me. You *have* kept it separately in the safe, right?"

"I have."

"Good. Then you just turn it over to me and don't list it on your quarterly P and L, okay? I'll take care of the publisher bills and the payment to the charity."

"Uh, okay," Bill replied. "But how do I account for the cash I took in and the cash I'm turning over to you?"

"Give it to me. Give me both the cash and the bills from the publisher and don't put it on the P and L. I'll do the rest."

"Okay, fine. I'll have the cash as well as the bills for you this afternoon."

The bishop abruptly switched the topic. “By the way, how did the interview with Lila Thompson go?”

Bill welcomed the question since he was more than happy to move on to a less stressful topic.

“Oh, fine. I hired her, and she’s starting next Monday.”

“Wonderful. So, I guess that wraps up our business for today.”

“Yes, sir. It does. Good afternoon.”

“Afternoon, Bill.”

Later, back in his office, Bill was carrying out the bishop’s bidding insofar as the cash and publisher invoices, but he felt uneasy as he did. Of course, the bishop was his boss, and he was obligated to do what he wanted, but it seemed a bit unorthodox.

When he had started his position as the manager, he was told that all the proceeds were to benefit the church. Were things falling apart somehow?

After a little more soul-searching, he concluded that it was none of his affair. The bishop was the boss, and whatever he wanted was what Bill would do. Still, the instructions gnawed at him. He eventually concluded that he would leave it in the hands of the Lord.

# CHAPTER FOUR

Lila was quite overjoyed to finally have employment and the hope of adequately supporting her kids. She lately found herself taking special attention to dressing for her part-time job at the bookstore. More than once, she chastised herself. *Girl, you'd think you were going out on a high school date instead of going to work.*

But that didn't stop her. She still took extra time with her choice of clothes, makeup, and accessories, reminding herself that when she was working or going to school, she had always taken care to dress appropriately and stylishly. She knew it was important to present herself as professionally as possible.

*Who knows?* She wondered. *This could lead to bigger, better opportunities.*

As usual, her aunt was on time to babysit, and Lila scurried off to work. She arrived at the bookstore fifteen minutes before it was time for her to clock in. Bill greeted her with a hearty good morning and welcomed her aboard.

After that, he began to show her around the store before training her. She noted that the store was adorned with memorabilia of Bishop Hines and inspirational artists—but far more of Bishop Hines. He explained the layout of the store, showing where to organize items on the shelves. The primary thing Lila had to do was direct people to whatever kind of book they were looking for. She didn't need much training as a sales clerk since she had done that kind of work before.

While the store specialized in religious books, especially those written by the current icons of the Christian church, they did carry other titles. Most of these were in the how-to category. They ranged from how to build a porch and how to pick a husband to how to start a home business. They even carried a religious and inspirational section comprised of both fiction and nonfictional titles.

Of course, Bishop Hines and Bill Pierce reviewed every book they sold. If it didn't violate any of the morals or precepts of True Faith Christian Church, it was generally ordered and stocked—that is, as long as a publisher's sales rep convinced Bill the book was selling well. The only other criterion was that it could be bought cheaply.

The bookstore itself, located on church property and in a building owned by the church, had low overhead. Most of the other staff members were volunteers that the bishop had cajoled into serving, and Lila was now one of the few paid workers. The low overhead meant that the store was able to offer good discounts. While many of the customers came from the True Faith Church's congregation, the other titles and the good discounts helped attract other clientele from the church's middle-class neighborhood.

The first day on the job, when Lila had called Bill Pierce "Mr. Pierce," he insisted that they worked in an informal shop and that she should call him Bill—never "boss" or "Mr. Pierce."

Lila never took her lunch break when Bill did, but occasionally he would pop into the next-door lunch counter for coffee when Lila was at lunch and join her. It was comfortable since they had their mutual interest in the store to talk about.

The last time he had talked to her about the part of his ministry that involved mentoring troubled parishioners, and they had some interesting talks about the state of modern society in America, especially the South.

Of course, Lila was careful to avoid discussing her own personal troubles. Having worked for Bill in the store, she couldn't imagine leaning on him for counsel regarding her personal home life too.

But she did learn some interesting things about Bill. He was married to his high school sweetheart; he had a bachelor's degree in theology with an emphasis on Christian studies; and he and his wife wanted to have two kids. He was interested in preaching and hoped one day to be able to do that.

Still, some of her own problems were soon revealed.

One afternoon when Bill was facing a deadline for an inventory and the volunteers were unable to show up, he asked Lila to work overtime. Lila called Marcie to see if she could stay a while longer with the kids. With the extra money she was making at the store, she could give Marcie something to help out with school expenses.

Bill had gone out to get them coffee for a break, and when he handed over her cup, he said, “I can’t tell you how much I appreciate this. In a way, it was my own fault for putting it off so long, but the church’s board of directors decided that they needed a financial statement for some new federal grant they were looking for. So, it kind of came out of the blue.”

Lila took a sip of coffee, smiled, and said, “No problem. I’m glad to help.”

The job consisted of running the computer sheets and making a physical tally of everything in the back storeroom. The front area was no problem since that inventory could be checked against the weekly sales sheets that listed every transaction by book title.

At one point in the afternoon, Bill found her deeply engrossed in one of the books. “Looks good,” he said, grinning.

She looked up, startled. “Oh, I’m sorry. This caught my eye, and I read the back cover…and before I knew it, I was hooked. I thought I might be able to learn something.”

“Which one is it?” Bill asked. “*How to Find the Right Mate*”?

She grinned. “It’s called *How to Raise Godly Children*.” Bill’s eyes caught hers, and the two broke out in a simultaneous giggle.

He said, "Darn, that's one book I'd love to have a need for."

Puzzled, Lila said, "They write books on how to do everything—how to live your life and who to marry—but they don't really write about how to deal with the things that split people up."

Bill's lids dropped. "I know. My ministry is supposed to be about helping people cope with life's unexpected problems."

Lila, sensing his melancholy, said, "And I bet you do a good job of it."

"You're too kind. But how can the teacher teach what he can't do himself?"

An awkward silence followed, and Lila then said, "Do you think they had the same problems—say, one or two generations back—like during our parents' and grandparents' times?"

Bill took a sip of coffee and thoughtfully replied, "Every generation has its own problems. In our parents' and grandparents' times, they had to deal with things like the Great Depression, poverty, and unfair social and employment stuff."

Lila raised her eyebrow. “Seems to me that a lot of that is still around.”

“True,” Bill said, “but today we have some insidious and tough problems like AIDS and drugs and teenage pregnancy.”

“You got that right.”

“Coming from my limited experience here at True Faith, I kind of look at some of today’s problems like a kind of nuclear radiation.”

Lila raised her eyebrow and blinked. “Nuclear radiation?”

“Exactly. Nuclear waste and radiation have what I call an eternal life. In other words, once we're exposed, we cannot be cleansed—at least not in one’s lifetime. I see drug addiction in the same way. Some addictions, like heroin, are almost impossible of curing. You don’t see many cured heroin addicts. Most die young. That’s what I mean by ‘almost impossible’ problems. But my main counseling advice is, ‘The Lord will see you through it.’ Jesus is our only hope, our only salvation.”

Suddenly, he seemed embarrassed. “Look at me giving a sermon.” He grinned. “Hey, I think we’re almost finished.”

Afterward he gave her a hug to show his appreciation. Lila came away from it feeling something, but wasn't quite sure exactly what it was.

The next day Bill approached her on a coffee break and said, "I really need to do something for you for being kind enough to help me out the other day."

She begged off graciously. "Don't be silly. I was glad to help."

"No. I will be silly. Would you like to join my wife and me at Stooge's Sports Bar? You know—over on Collins Road, near Route 285?"

She put her hand to her throat, which she always did when she was nervous, and hesitated.

"Listen," he said. "I'm a Georgia Tech fan. They have this huge thirty-six-inch TV screen, and they're going to be showing the Georgia Tech/Gators game. The Buffalo wings and fries aren't bad, either —but then again, how many places could mess up wings and fries?"

"I…I don't know. You say your wife's going?"

"She's not much of a sports fan, but she promised. What do

you say?"

His enthusiasm was contagious, and she didn't want to appear ungrateful or stuffy, so she agreed.

It was late Friday afternoon, a happy time for most workers, when they piled in Bill's modest compact and headed for Stooge's in Atlanta. On the way, Lila asked, "Is your wife going to meet us there?"

"That's what she promised."

Stooge's was a low-slung white building with a long red canopy leading to the front door, and Bill was right; the root beer and appetizers were great. They settled into a booth and ordered as they chatted and awaited the start of the game.

A short time later, they were happily eating pigs in blankets, fries, and hot wings. The game was a good one, but what Lila mainly noticed was that Bill never once took his eyes off the screen to check for his wife's arrival. She tried to mention it a few times, but each time she did the Gators scored a touchdown and the booing muted her voice.

Soon Lila was drawn into the game herself. On one occasion,

the officials began to argue over a critical play, stirring excitement everywhere. While they waited on the replay to help decide it, Lila gave her expert take on the play, at least based on her knowledge of basketball.

Afterward Bill turned to her. “How did you become such a basketball aficionado?” he asked.

“My ex was a basketball player.”

“Oh, that’s right. I think you told me. So, you’ve got to love basketball then, right?”

“I wouldn’t say *love* it. In some ways, basketball seems to be at the root of me and my ex’s problems.”

“How so?” he asked with a frown. But before she could answer, the replay appeared, and the roar from the local crowd again blocked out her answer.

Bill’s wife never showed up, and by the time they were almost ready to leave, Lila mentioned it again. Bill replied, “Oh, yeah. I wonder what happened.”

He pulled out his cell phone and turned away to dial. A few minutes later, he turned back to her and said, “She couldn’t make it. Something came up." Without missing a beat, he asked, "Would you like something else to eat or drink? I'm stuffed."

"Oh, no, I'm good."

Just as they were headed out the door, Lila heard a familiar scream.

"Girl? Girl? Is that you?"

It was Desiree. She was with two burly college men who looked like football players.

Lila was struggling for words. She knew she had to introduce her to Bill, and she also knew how it looked.

"Hi, Desiree. Yes, I'm here with my boss. Bill, this is my friend, Desiree. Desiree, this is my boss at the bookstore, Bill Pierce."

Desiree leaned forward and, rejecting his outstretched hand, kissed him on the cheek. She said, "How you doin', handsome?" even as she threw Lila a conspiratorial wink.

Lila was about to speak when Desiree said, "Hey, why don't y'all come with us. We're going to a karaoke bar. You know how you love to karaoke, girl. At least you used to," she added.

Lila immediately turned away without looking at Bill, who hadn't said yes or no. So Desiree addressed the question to him. "What ya say? Take this party pooper homey of mine and convince her to come along with us."

Now it was Bill who was about to speak, and Lila said, "No, no, Desiree. I've got to get home. I have a babysitter to relieve. I simply can't."

Desiree looked at Bill, who shrugged somewhat helplessly. Even though Lila had a wonderful time, she was suspicious about Bill's wife and the reasons for her not showing up. She was no star-struck teenager who believed everything a man told her. She felt that she knew men well enough to know that even the best of them will succumb to things they might not ordinarily when they are having problems at home.

And then she had to deal with Desiree when they spoke on Saturday afternoon. Desiree wouldn't let her admit that it was an innocent thing. "Yeah, girl. You go right on tellin' me that, but this ole girl knows better. He was kind of a cute guy," she said, before adding, "but you never told me you dated white guys."

The whole episode felt unseemly. It bothered Lila so much that on Monday afternoon, just before quitting time, she asked, "Bill, were you being straight with me about your wife coming to Stooge's with us?"

It was clear he was acting guilty.

"You'd think less of me if I lied, so I'm going to tell you the truth. I did ask her, but she changed her mind at the last minute. I knew you wouldn't agree if I didn't tell you my wife would be coming, and I honestly saw nothing wrong with us having some fun."

Lila lowered her eyes. "Still, Bill, that was dishonest, and I don't want to come between a man and his wife. I don't want to refuse to do something like that again, but unless I have assurances, I won't go out with you again either."

His face reddened, and he began shuffling like a schoolboy. "Lila, I'm sorry, and I won't do it again. In fact, I would never do anything to harm our friendship. I'm sorry, but you've got to believe me when I say it was innocent."

"Maybe it was, Bill. But the fact is you're a married man, and

I'm a single woman, and it's just not right."

She also wanted to mention that he was white but decided that would be so not cool. After all, this is the twenty-first century.

# CHAPTER FIVE

Bill asked Lila to manage the bookstore for two days while he attended a media seminar, and Lila had no problem proving her worth by holding things down on her own. Finding babysitters was never an easy task but she needed the extra money, which made the task less burdensome.

She was totally immersed in bagging a sale for a customer and answering two phone calls at the same time when she sensed someone standing in front of her. Heavenly cologne circulating in the air hinted to his identity before she looked up to confirm it. But as she did, she immediately noticed Bishop Hines's glowing smile enveloped inside his devilishly handsome face.

"Good morning to you, sister. How are you with the Lord today?"

"Oh, hi, Bishop. Just fine, thanks."

One thing about Bishop Hines was that he didn't just flash a smile. He held it like a floating feather defies gravity, and it made her feel like she was relished in a glowing sun, needing only to bask in the warmth of it. Yes, indeed, he was mesmerizing.

"Where's our manager today? And shame on him for letting such a pretty little thing work so hard."

Lila smiled and acknowledged him. "He's at a media seminar, and everything is going well. It was me who volunteered to run the store while he's gone, but we both agreed that his learning more about media was well worth my time."

"So I take it you're really busy."

Pushing some of her hair out of her eyes, she replied, "Yes, I am, but I can handle it."

"Good, because I don't want you to worry your pretty head about it," the bishop said. "I wanted to talk to him about book sales."

With a smile of her own, she replied, "I have to tell you, Bishop. Ever since your appearance on the Christian network, sales of your book have been skyrocketing!"

The bishop's smile grew even wider. "My, my, that's encouraging. Praise the Lord."

"Praise Him," Lila agreed.

"Let's celebrate the good news. Why don't you take a break and let me buy you lunch?"

"I wish I could, but my volunteer help is late and I can't leave the store unattended."

"No, of course not."

He held her attention for a moment before saying, "How about me bringing you back some tea or a lunch or…whatever you like?"

"That would be fine. It usually slows down right about now, so maybe it would be a good time to have lunch," she said while fishing in her purse for money.

Hines put his hand out in a gesture for her to stop. "Please. No need for that, my dear. It's my treat. What would you like?"

"Tea and one of those blueberry scones would be nice."

"Comin' right up," he said, and he scurried away but not before displaying that signature white smile of his, of course.

Lila noticed a slew of meddling heads turn as he left, but she ignored them.

She had hardly been back to work for a mere few minutes

when the bishop returned. They engaged in small talk as they ate, and it pleased her that he showed her so much attention. While stirring her tea behind the counter, Bishop Hines leaned forward, placed his elbows on the counter, and positioned himself closer to Lila as they spoke. Lila instinctively moved back a bit. She instantly realized that this handsome man was intimidating, and she had a sense that he realized it too.

Drinking his tea and munching on a large buttered roll he mused, "I shouldn't have this tea roll, but I just couldn't resist it."

"Why? Are you worried about the cholesterol?"

"Oh, no," he replied while shaking his head in futility. "It's my weight," he acknowledged, only this time with a more serious expression.

She eyed him closely, desperately hoping to avoid a natural look of admiration in her eyes. "Come on, you're not the least bit heavy, Bishop."

"Why, thank you, sister." His face lit up in appreciation at the unveiled compliment. "I'll tell my doctor you said that the next time I see him." He took another sip of tea and a bite of the coffee roll and said, "So how do you like your job? I *so* hoped that it would work out for you, but I hate to see you overburdened like this."

Lila's face brightened. "Oh…It's no problem, especially when you love your work. And I must say I love it."

"Great. Listen, I understand it was you and Bill who discussed my going on the Christian network to get my message across to new parishioners and push my book."

Lila reached for a strand of hair so nervously that any strand would do. "Well, it was originally Bill's idea, and after we talked it over, it seemed like a good one. I mentioned how someone like Oprah could send an author's book sales up the charts. Really. I couldn't see *anything* but good coming from it."

"That's true. Indeed it was helpful, sister; indeed it was."

"In fact," Lila added, "no doubt that media exposure helps sales, so I'm sure the seminar he is at will be useful too."

"I can see that. But I think that as far as television goes, it's more about how you look than what you say."

She furrowed her brow, thinking about that one. "Actually, I'm not sure. I have a feeling it's a bit of both."

With a twinkle in his eyes, the bishop asked, "What did you think? Personally, I mean."

"Well…I…uh…"

Just then, a customer walked up to the counter with a copy of Bishop Hines's new book clutched to her bosom like a valued treasure. It was Bessie. She was an elderly woman, one of the well-respected mothers of the church and local community; everyone knew her. She had known the bishop's parents when they were alive and had joined the ministry when he only had a few members. Bessie was an instrumental part of getting various programs started in the church. Upon recognizing her, the bishop's demeanor became somewhat childlike.

"Oh, hello, Bishop," she said. "I'm surely looking forward to reading your book. I hear that it's simply wonderful. So many people have told me that."

Lila figured that the bishop was thinking how important it was to have her approval, as others in the church would call upon her critique.

"Bless you, Mother Bessie. Bless you. I pray it is to your liking."

Bessie dawdled far longer than was necessary to complete her purchase, inventing idle chatter. She seemed to make the bishop uneasy, as though he were in the presence of royalty. When it came to Mother Bessie, he didn't appear to mind the interruption of his conversation with Lila. Mother Bessie was clearly so happy to be with the bishop. She would surely be telling her friends all about it this afternoon.

When she finally left, Bishop Hines said, "Mother Bessie loves to talk, the old dear."

"Yeah, she's been saving up for the book."

"Bless her heart," he said. Then he turned back to Lila. To regain control of his composure and the conversation, he said, "I think you were going to comment on something?"

Lila was surprised to see the bishop in such a humble state. "Oh, no…It's nothing."

"You can speak freely my child," he said, his voice full of mirth. "I always welcome feedback from my parishioners."

"I was just trying to understand how your remarks on television squared with your recent sermon. You know, when you informed the congregation that you would no longer accept a salary, but instead accept whatever their charity allowed in place of it."

She could tell that she had his full attention now. It was as though he had switched into business mode. "Go on," he encouraged her.

Lila swallowed hard before continuing, but her curiosity was getting the best of her now. "On television, you said that a preacher's salary should be God's will. Whatever He willed is what you should accept."

Hines seemed puzzled. "Yes?"

"Well, what I don't understand is that you told the congregation that you couldn't live on what you were earning as the pastor, and that you would be willing to accept whatever charity they could afford to give."

"That is correct." His tone was polite yet firm. "Well, aren't you guaranteeing yourself a pay cut?"

Without hesitating, the bishop again flashed his trademark

smile. “I’m sure one might think that if one didn’t have faith in Christians and our congregation in the manner that I do.”

Now it was Lila’s turn to be puzzled.

Hines seemed to see it in her eyes, and he responded right away. “No need to worry about me, sister. I am now earning almost twice what I was earning from my salary. One just needs to ask people to dig down deep, and more times than not, they will do just that.”

Lila cocked her head. “But I thought the idea was to leave it up to the Lord—let Him decide what your compensation would be. I thought the idea was that God would be the final paymaster.”

“Who’s to say that my new method of getting paid is not the Lord’s will? If it’s not His will, whose will is it?”

Lila had to think that over.

“Do you see?” he asked, his tone as sincere as his Sunday preaching voice. Few could find anything disingenuous in it. His face and demeanor were the epitome of honesty.

While she didn’t really understand, there seemed to be no point in discussing it further. Besides, she didn’t have the time or the energy to dwell on such lofty topics just then. In a way, she was a little embarrassed that she'd brought it up in the first place.

Lila recalled a very interesting lesson in Bible school, which says that if you feel that the Lord is not listening to your prayers, then you aren't being faithful enough. And if you aren't financially prosperous, your salvation must be questioned. She had heard the philosophy called, rather derisively, "name it and claim it."

He had been unable to keep the sly look off his face as he told her that he had actually doubled his salary when everyone thought he was being a martyr and accepting less.

Her hand was dwarfed when he took it in his. He then patted it and said, "Well, this has been the most pleasant lunch I've had in a while, but I have to get back. Ask Bill to give me a call when he returns."

"Of course, Bishop," she replied, smiling graciously. "Have a nice afternoon."

When Lila got home, Desiree was sitting in her living room, bouncing Royal on her knee. The child was delighting in the attention and screaming with glee. Lila took the rambunctious toddler and said, “Desiree, you’re going to spoil that child. I’ll never get him down for his nap now.”

“Hush up, girl. You wanna make sure he don’t have no fun at all. For goodness’ sake, he’ll wind up as dull as you.”

Lila grinned. “Heaven forbid.” She took the cooing child and continued to play with him.

Desiree said, “So?”

“So what?”

“So what’s goin’ on with this white dude—your boss?”

“Going on? We were watching the game.”

“Yeah, right. So you say, but I sense some *Jungle Fever* going on there.”

Lila could feel herself blushing. “Oh, Desiree, you are terrible. It’s no such thing.”

“I hear from some sisters that he is free.”

“Yeah, right,” Lila said with a giggle. “His wife was supposed to join us, but something happened.”

Desiree shook her head and smiled impishly. “Sure. Sure she was. Like I said, I hear he’s a free man.”

"Where would you hear that?" Lila demanded, raising her voice.

"Don't matter where I heard it. That guy is a free man, I tell you."

Putting the baby back down in his crib, Lila said, "Well, even if he is, it makes no difference to me."

Desiree rolled her eyes. "Pray tell, why is that? I'm not saying he's the greatest catch, but at least he'd be a man on your arm."

Lila didn't like where this conversation was going. "Desiree, we've been all over this. When I'm ready, I'll do my own matchmaking, thank you. Besides, all Bill wanted to do was to see the game."

"Really? Then answer me this."

*Here we go,* Lila thought, as she waited for what she knew was her friend's inevitable question.

"Why couldn't you guys go watch it in the church social activities room with everyone else?" Desiree inquired.

"Don't be silly, Desiree. You know working people like to go out on Friday night and have some fun. The activities room is no place for having fun and being with other adults. It's usually filled with a bunch of rowdy kids."

Desiree again unleashed her impish smile. "Really? What did you find at Stooges? Let me guess—rowdy adults?"

"Yes," Lila shot back. "But not us. It was completely innocent."

"Uh-huh," Desiree said, patronizing her friend. "You keep thinking that, Lila. Girl, don't you know nothin' about men?"

The two stared at each other in an awkward silence. Soon after, Desiree assessed her friend more seriously, before saying, "You know, I take it back. Knowing you, it probably was all innocent." She shook her head and sighed. "All my influence goes nowhere with you. I must be wasting my time. You've learned nothin'."

Lila could only grin at her friend's ranting. But she had to admit that even being linked with a man, although innocent, was fun. She and Lamont had been divorced for a year and a half, and even though she made light of it, the information that perhaps Bill was now single intrigued her in a way. It planted a seed of some kind in the far corners of her psyche, for this was the first time since the divorce that she ever had an inclination that she could be happy in a relationship.

In any case, the very thought gave her a little tingle of hope and eagerness that she hadn't experienced in a long time. It wasn't that Bill was such a catch; it was simply the idea of having friendship and interaction with a man.

She, of course, kept this bit of elation to herself, even though she seriously doubted that she could hide it from Desiree for long. Desiree was a fox that could smell a chicken in a hen house a mile away, and Lila was such an amateur at the dating game it almost scared her.

# CHAPTER SIX

Lila took pride in maintaining her privacy. She wasn't usually one to put her business in the street, and she didn't like to pry into other people's affairs. However, she couldn't help but notice that Bill, now her boss and good friend, was extremely depressed. They had been eating lunch together almost every day, but he said nothing to indicate that something was going on.

However, by closing time on Friday afternoon, he was so depressed that Lila felt she would be negligent if she didn't ask.

"What's wrong, Bill?" she asked. "You seem awfully down today."

To his credit, Bill hadn't whined to her or anybody in the store about his problems. He simply said, "I'm sorry if I'm a downer. I know I am."

"Don't be silly, Bill. Everybody has problems."

"Yeah, but I don't want to bore anybody with mine. Sorry if I have a hard time hiding it."

She lowered her eyes a bit, which prompted a question from him: “What? Did I say something to…?”

“No, Bill, it’s just that I thought you may need someone to talk to. I know we don’t know a lot about each other, but we have shared a few things, and I feel bad that you feel you can’t talk to me.”

Bill brightened up. “Oh, gosh! I’m sorry. I don’t want you to feel that way. Like I said, I just don’t wanna burden others with my problems.”

She turned to go out the door. “Okay, I’ll see you Monday. But please remember what I said.”

“Thanks, Lila. I will. Have a nice weekend.”

"You too. Just remember the Lord doesn’t put any more on us than we can bear.”

“I know. Thanks for reminding me. Maybe I should work harder at trying to get on with my life.”

Lila had an idea of what he was talking about but didn’t think it was the right time to ask him. Unfortunately, she knew all about marital despair.

Monday, at lunch, as they sat down in the back room where they usually ate, he didn't seem any better. Lila said, "My aunt made me three sandwiches. She thinks I'm too skinny."

He gazed at her as she unwrapped one of the sandwiches. "What kind are they?"

"Meat loaf with tomato sauce. Want one?"

He grinned, probably for the first time in months. "How did you know I love meat loaf?"

"Please have one. I can't eat more than one."

"Be happy to oblige," he said, unwrapping his and taking a bite. He grinned. "Tell your aunt I want to marry her."

They laughed and dug into the sandwiches. After eating, they sipped Cokes, and she said, "I hope you feel that you can talk to me if you need to."

He gazed into her eyes, seemingly thinking about what she said. "I know," he said, "and I will if I need to. Thanks for being a friend."

She resisted an urge to hug him as they went back to work. Bill's spirits seemed to be up for a while, but by week's end, he was in a major funk again.

Lila, feeling her own need to share, said, “Bill, if you don’t let me help, I’m going to be mad at you.”

He looked like a lost doe as he took a deep breath, exhaled, and said, “My life is in shambles.”

Lila released a sigh as he finally opened to her.

“My wife wants a divorce, and I have no idea why.” He was whispering and looking woefully at Lila. “Nobody can help me, Lila. I’m in a hell of my own making.”

“I know this must be hard for you.” Lila, however, was not shocked at his admission because of the rumors she had heard around the church. “Have you asked the Lord to help?”

“Oh, yes. He doesn’t seem to know either.”

“What does Renee tell you?”

He stared at her blankly. “She just says that she doesn’t feel anything for me anymore.”

Lila earnestly said, “Isn’t that something that lots of couples go through from time to time? Isn’t that something counseling might help?”

"We tried counseling."

"And?" she asked.

"It solved nothing. The counselor couldn't get to the bottom of it."

"Well, you mean not yet."

"Yeah, I guess so," he said, "though we haven't scheduled any more meetings."

She waited for him to continue, almost feeling a bit like a counselor herself now.

He said, "We tried all the counselor's little suggestions—like things to put the spark back in our marriage."

"Like romantic dinners or a change of pace…maybe new hobbies? Those sorts of things?" Lila inquired with a tone of understanding.

"Right. But it all seemed so contrived and hokey. It just made us feel awkward, as if we were trying to follow a recipe for happiness. And I'm not sure there is such a thing."

"Those things work for a lot of people," she said, trying to be encouraging.

"I guess." He looked at her and veiled a small grin. "She even suggested that Renee try dressing a little differently."

Lila couldn't hide her surprise. "Differently? I've recognized Renee from the picture on your desk, and she dresses very, uh, appropriately, I think."

"Yeah, maybe for church, but I'm sure the counselor was thinking of ways to spice up our marriage."

Now Lila raised an eyebrow. "Did Renee always dress, uh, appropriately?"

"No, not before we both got active in the church.

It's almost as if she thinks God is watching and will disapprove of her dressing any other way than how she does."

"What do you think?"

"I think the Lord wants us to be comfortable in our dress—not cheap, of course—but a woman doesn't have to be trashy in order to be attractive and stylish."

When she caught his gaze to see if he was getting her point, she mumbled awkwardly, "She just has to dress stylishly."

"This is just one of the problems. I know talking about

someone's clothing style is trivial, and that's how people become when they have fallen out of love."

"You're right, Bill. It is trivial, and maybe you have fallen out of love or have outgrown each other. But you all have to search out the real problem before throwing in the towel."

He shrugged. "I don't know, but the difference between her and me is that I'm willing to try to work it out. She doesn't seem to want to."

After a long pause, Lila said, "I don't want to be negative, but is there a chance that Renee is seeing someone else?"

"I have no idea." He spoke with what seemed to be little interest. "Renee," he said thoughtfully, "seems to think that if we had kids, it would have bonded us more and made us closer."

Lila said, "What do you think?"

"I don't know if that's true. If two people aren't in love anymore, how could bringing innocent children into the world help that, right?"

Lila said seriously, "I know firsthand that kids are not the glue that holds a man and a woman together. They have to be willing to make the marriage work for themselves. Kids may prolong the inevitable, but they cannot keep two people together." Lila paused briefly, drifting into the thought that she and Royal would somehow stop Lamont from using drugs.

Then she suddenly said, "Besides, she probably doesn't want to do that now, unless you guys patch things up."

Bill said, "I think that while love is a universal emotion, people are different in their attitudes about it. Some think it should be a forever thing, and so they get married. Others are sure it is not a forever thing and that they can be in love many times in their lives. That is probably more of a male attitude than a female one. But I think that a man can be just as romantic as a woman and believe that love is truly a forever thing."

Lila thought about that for a long moment before answering.

"I think that's a male myth. Women are just as capable of thinking the same thing, although few would admit it. It's just that some people feel that when they take those vows, it becomes less about love and romance and more about the piece of paper you sign, as though you are signing away your life or gaining ownership of a piece of property or something."

He lowered his eyes. "How do you feel about that?"

"I'm not sure. I'm so confused at this point in my life that I can't offer any constructive advice. All I can offer is a shoulder and a ready ear to listen."

"Another lost soul," he lamented.

Lila chewed her lower lip for a moment. "Haven't you and Renee been together since high school?"

"Yeah, just like you."

Lila was a bit taken aback since she had never discussed her marriage and divorce with anybody but Desiree. "How did you know that?" she asked timidly.

"You must have told me."

"I don't think so."

"Then it must have been the bishop. Maybe it was when we discussed your coming to work here."

"Oh," she said.

Bill said, "Will you tell me the truth about something?"

"If I can."

"Your aunt didn't really make you three meat loaf sandwiches last week—did she?"

Now she felt chagrined and trapped. "No. I know you like meat loaf. I just wanted to cheer you up."

"Well, no need to apologize, and I'm sorry if I embarrassed you. But that was a sweet thing to do."

Lila was just pleased to be a friendly sounding board for him. It had been a while since she had had this kind of conversation with a man. She understood his pain, and it made her feel like a helpful Christian to listen to him. She felt as if they were good friends. As she examined how she was feeling, she could sense that she wanted something more, but she didn't dare think about what it could be.

Bill and Lila shared more information about each other over the months, and they became each other's confidants. Bill also became involved in Lila's life in some unexpected ways. When she had problems getting herself to work or the kids to school, he would step in and help.

And so he was introduced to her kids. He said, "Royal—what a different name."

Lila smiled. "When he was born, someone said he looked like a little prince, so I named him Royal."

"And this little guy here—what's his name?"

Jackson hid behind his mother's leg and only peeked out once.

Lila said, "This here's Jackson. And that young lady over there gawking at you is little Latoya."

Bill kneeled down to their level and said, "Hey, would you guys like to see my egg trick?"

Jackson stepped out from behind Lila's leg. "What?" he asked.

"You know, my egg trick.—just watch!" Grinning, Bill walked gingerly to the refrigerator and found an egg. As he walked back to the living room coffee table, the children looked on in anticipation. "I can make this egg stand up on its pointy end."

He showed them how the egg rolled over when he tried to stand it up on the table. "Yes, I can make it stand up."

"Can not!" Jackson said while Latoya just giggled.

"I'll bet you a nickel," Bill said. Jackson replied, "Ain't got a nickel."

"Well, I'll lend you one." He fished out two nickels from his pocket and gave them each one. Latoya promptly ran away with hers.

Bill laughed. "Jackson mentioned that she's only a kid."

"Okay, put up your nickel and I'll put up mine," Bill said, grinning. "Remember, the bet is that I can make this egg stand up on its pointy end."

"Can not."

"Can too. Watch."

Bill made a fist, leaving a small opening. He stuck the pointy end of the egg inside the small hole at the index finger. He held it in the air.

"Ta-daaaaa," he crowed, and the kids howled with laughter.

Jackson frowned. "That's not magic. That's just a trick. You're holding it up."

"Yeah," he responded. "I told you I could make it stand up."

Bill gained two new fans after his amateur trick. The kids liked him, and whenever Lila had some kind of transportation problem with the kids, he was there. Her car routinely broke down after that, and she couldn't afford to take it to the garage. However, Bill was always there with the parts and the help of a mechanic friend to repair it for her in her own driveway.

His help was truly a godsend, because she had no way to fix the car. And Lord knows that she couldn't keep her job if she couldn't get to work. For the first time, she began to think about where she would be without him.

*These were simply things that friends did for each other*, she thought. Just like in times past, when Lila sometimes relied on Desiree to come to her aid with a loan, or her time.

After work, Lila saw Des standing outside of the bookstore. She was delighted to see her. Lila had been keeping long hours at the bookstore, leaving her little time left to socialize.

Des fired off at Lila right away. "Hey, girl, what's been up with you? Can a 'sistah' get a return phone call or what? You do remember that we're supposed to be friends, don't you? Well, don't you?"

Lila laughed as she hugged her friend. "Yes, girl, and I've missed you too. I'm sorry—I've have been meaning to call you.

It's been so busy at the bookstore, and they've increased my hours."

"Well, that's good to know 'cause I thought you kicked me to the curb."

"No, silly, I could never do that."

"Then how come you don't come to me when you got problems?"

"Well," Lila stalled, "I know you sleep late and all, and there is nothing you can do about a broken car."

"Come on, girl. I could loan you some money and you know it."

"Oh, Desiree, I owe you enough already."

"Uh-huh," she said in her sly "baloney" voice.

"What does that mean?"

"What does it usually mean? I think you got eyes for that deacon fellow. What's his name?"

"His name is Bill."

"I can see how *that* was on the tip of your tongue for sure."

"Oh, Desiree. You are so quick to judge people," she said with mock annoyance, knowing that she was unable to hide a thing from her shrewd girlfriend.

"Girl, I only judge you 'cause I know you. I always knew you wanted a man. I'm just happy I know who he is now."

Lila didn't bother to argue, since doing so would make it appear that she was guilty of something. Although Des was partly right, Lila kept her friendship with Bill as confidential as possible.

Over the next few months, Bill and Lila continued to confide in each other about their lives. Lila talked about her past travails with Lamont, while Bill tried to make sense of what was happening between him and Renee. The more he talked with Lila, the less depressed he became about the situation.

One day Bill dropped the bomb by informing her that they had been seeing an attorney to finalize the divorce.

"It was inevitable that Renee and I would end up at the crossroad of our marriage," he explained to her. "I've tried to make things work with Renee, but *she* thinks it's best that we get a divorce."

"But Bill, are you sure about this?" Lila asked sadly. "You

can't make a hasty decision on something this serious."

"It's not a hasty decision, at least on my part. And what can I do now anyway? I think we *both* somehow knew that it wasn't going to work a long time ago, without even mentioning it. We're just facing the fact that we're both miserable."

"Have you informed Bishop Hines?" Lila asked.

"Yes, I have, and he and I agreed that this is the best decision, given our situation."

"Really?"

This didn't sit well with Lila. After all, it *was* Bill's wife who was unyielding and wanting the divorce, she reasoned. Knowing that Bill didn't initiate the proceeding made her feel better about the situation, but she also cursed the devil for making her almost feel darn good.

# CHAPTER SEVEN

Bill became a single man in no time, it seemed. Lila could finally exhale about being seen with him in public, but she still had her reservations. Lila was sweet and sensitive and wanted to take things slowly. She hoped and prayed that Bill wouldn't take to the races by getting aggressively romantic. She went out of her way to keep things from getting steamy, even steering away from intimate dinners and evenings alone in front of the TV. Not that he had really been moving in that direction —he hadn't—but he was a man, and she feared that Bill *could* be expecting far more than she was prepared to give.

Without thinking of it or planning for it to be, Bill was becoming a familiar part of her family. Her Aunt Nona and her kids liked him especially, but Aunt Nona was wary too. She was old school and therefore raised her eyebrows the minute Bill told Lila that he was officially divorced from his wife.

Just as Lila's mom had often done, Aunt Nona always spoke in parables to Lila. At the dinner table one day, she blurted out, "Chile, you know, when cars move too fast, it's hard to see who's behind the wheel. But if you follow slowly behind it and wait 'til it stops, you can see clearly inside—and then you'll know just who's driving."

With respect, Lila said, "Yes, ma'am," knowing exactly what her point was.

The truth was she hadn't given much thought to what she wanted from Bill even with Desiree's urging. She wasn't even sure she wanted a relationship or an affair.

Lila had to be tricky and agile to escape his attempts at good-night kisses though, letting him get away with only a peck on the cheek before she hastily retreated through her front door and into the sanctuary of her apartment. Sometimes, after evading him once again, she would stand with her back against the closed front door, wondering how long she could put him off—or if she even wanted to.

Of course, Desiree chided her for this. "Girl, what you waiting for?" she asked one afternoon as they were chatting in Lila's living room. “Time is movin’ on and you ‘ain’t gettin’ no younger.”

Lila simply shrugged. “There’s no need to hurry things.”

“You like the man, don’t you? And if not, what you even going out with him for?”

“It’s not that…nothing like that. It’s just that I’m new to this, and I prefer to take it slow.”

“You sure it ain’t got nothin’ to do with him being white and all?”

Lila cocked her head. “And all what?”

“I don’t know. You tell me!”

“Well, I’ll admit that this interracial stuff is kind of worrisome. I’ve never even thought out the possibility. But yeah, it is worrisome—that’s for sure.”

“Only if you plan to marry the man.”

“Well, I don’t see that in the future.”

Now it was Desiree’s turn to cock her head. “I don’t know why the hell not?”

Lila had to think a bit. “I don’t know either. I’m just not

thinking along those lines."

Desiree flipped her hair and put on her lipstick. As she did, she made a lip-biting motion to spread it, grinned, and said, "I suppose that means that he hasn't rocked your world yet."

Lila grinned back, enjoying the female give-and-take. "It's way too early for that, girl. Way too early. I'm not even sure I want to."

"And why not?"

This time she was quick to say, "I don't know, Desiree. I don't know."

"You got needs, don't you girl?"

"Of course I do. I'm just as human as the next person is. But I have to feel something emotionally too. I can't just cater to the needs of my body. The Lord tells us about that."

Desiree rolled her eyes. "I figured," she said, shaking out her hair. "What's so wrong about that? Men have been doing it for eons. Haven't you heard about women's lib? It's all the rage nowadays. Like I said, men do it all the time."

"I'm not a man, and I don't care what others do anyway," Lila retorted a bit defensively. “I have to be the way I was taught to be.”

Desiree rolled her eyes. “And nothing else?”

“That’s right,” she cooed, “nothing else.”

That evening Lila had trouble getting a babysitter, and she was outdone when she had to call Bill and tell him their date was off.

She could feel the anxiety in Bill’s reaction too.

“Hey, look,” he began, “I really want to see you, Lila. Why don’t I pick up a pizza—half onion for you—and a DVD? Name your flick.”

She agreed, giving him the title of the latest romantic comedy to pick up. Before Bill arrived, Lila read the kids a story and put them to bed.

Like a doting teenager, he greeted her at the door with a big smile and a kiss on the cheek. She tried her best to conceal her excitement as she greeted him with a warm hug. They were having a good time munching pizza, with Lila taking only small bites.

She recalled what her mother had told her about manners and being ladylike. “When you are eating dinner with a man, he wants to know that a lady has some home training," she would often say. With this thought, she gently wiped the corners of her mouth and placed her napkin back into her lap.

However, these days Lila usually ate on the run, only thinking of getting where she was going and what she had to do when she got there. When at home with the kids, she usually was too busy getting them to eat and hoping they didn't make a mess as she held Royal in her arms. This night was a pleasant change for Lila, however.

The movie was good, and Bill and Lila laughed the night away. They were becoming a couple while discovering a new level of comfort with each other. There was an ease about them now that they were completely relaxed. The foundation for romantic love was finally in place.

A dollop of cheese lay on the corner of Lila's mouth as Bill leaned in with a napkin, murmuring, "Let me get that." He dabbed at her mouth and leaned in even closer, suddenly finding their lips only inches apart. Their eyes locked. Lila started to draw back, but he kept moving closer until their lips touched.

The sensation was intense. Lila hadn't been kissed in a long time, so naturally the kiss lingered. Neither drew back for it was no mistake. Both seemed lost in some surreal fantasy world of sensation. When their tongues began swimming madly back and forth, she broke off, panting a bit, and whispered, "I'm sorry, Bill. I'm just not—"

"No, Lila, don't apologize. It's me," Bill interrupted. Sorry. I—I meant no offense. We were having such a good time. I hope I haven't spoiled it."

"Of course not." Lila smiled before taking his hand.

But they couldn't get back into the movie, and Lila was sure that his senses were as heightened as hers were by now. Bill was fidgeting with the remote and was obviously perspiring. She blushed when she saw him wipe sweat from his brow and asked if she could turn on the ceiling fan.

"Yes," he replied. "A little cool air would be great right about now." They both laughed.

Lila tried to spark some conversation, but that soon began to lag. Then she said, "You know, I hate to bring this up."

Bill was a bit startled, hoping there wasn't something else between them. "What, Lila?"

She lowered her head. "Gee, I feel funny even thinking about it."

"Funny how?"

"A disloyal kind of funny, I guess. Have you noticed a common theme in the bishop's sermon lately?"

"Like what?" Bill asked, his eyes searching.

"Well," she replied, appearing somewhat guilty, "do you remember the bishop's message from last week's services?"

"I remember."

"Do you really?"

"Possibly. Let me see. It was from Malachi. Something like this, 'Bring all the tithe into the storehouse, that there be meat in mine house, and prove me now herewith, sayeth the Lord.'"

"Right," said Lila. "And the rest is, 'See if I will not open for you the windows of heaven and pour out for you a blessing until it overflows.'"

"And?" Bill asked in hope he would understand more fully.

"Well, he seems to be hitting all the arguments about the necessity of giving more than ever these days. The week before last, he was preaching about something very similar. Remember, he was teaching on the opening of John's third epistle: 'Beloved, I pray that you may prosper in all things and be in health, just as your soul prospers'?"

"What exactly are you getting at, Lila?" asked Bill.

"Alright. What's troubling me is the constant financial theme. It's like he doesn't want his congregation to forget that the Lord expects us to support His church and His ministers."

"Okay, go on," he said. "And like any salesman, he doesn't tell the whole story or flip to the other side of the coin."

"You mean the fact that those passages could be interpreted differently," he said. "That maybe they don't necessarily mean exactly what the bishop says they mean."

"Exactly," Lila said. "For example, Ecclesiastes…I think it's 9:11. Let me see. It goes something like…'I have seen something else under the sun. The race is not to the swift or the battle to the strong, neither yet bread to the wise, nor yet riches to men of understanding, nor yet favor to men of skill; but *time and chance* happen to them all.' Doesn't this seem to indicate that health and wealth don't necessarily show either God's favor or disfavor? After all, the Bible also says that during his time on this earth, Jesus didn't even have a place to lay His head."

"I know what you're saying," Bill said. "The bishop does always seem to be on the same theme lately. And always relating it back to money."

Lila sighed.

"So," Bill said, looking her directly in the eyes, "you've been thinking about this for a while, haven't you?"

She studied him and asked, "Is there something that you know that I don't know? Did he mention something to you about not making enough pay? Is that why he's always going on about money these days?"

Bill hesitated, weighing his thoughts before speaking. "No, actually, I understand that he is now earning, from tithes, more than twice what he used to get when the church was paying his salary. It's not like getting paid from tithes is wrong. What I question is the fact that he switched to this method instead of a salary. I think he's sly enough to know that he could get more by"—he paused for a moment—'squeezing people's consciences'?"

"I see what you mean. That doesn't leave a good taste in my mouth."

"Mine either," he said.

"I have to be honest with you, Bill. There is something else that I was wondering about too, but I probably would never bring it up were it not for this conversation."

He gazed at her with anticipation. He said, "And that is?"

"Well, it's the way he handles his book sales. From the presentation of the book to—"

Before she could go on, he finished her thought, saying, "And the way it takes preference over every other book in the store."

She nodded. "Yes, that too."

"What else?" Bill asked.

"The way he handles his book payments."

"Even I don't know what he is doing with that," Bill said with amazement.

“What is he doing? It’s all so hush-hush. He handles *everything* about the sales, from ordering to payments. Why is that Bill?”

“Well, I assumed that since it’s his book and he’s the head of our church, it gives him the right to handle it any way he wants.”

Bill chewed his lip, feeling uneasy about questioning the bishop’s integrity. “Yeah. I see what you mean. I don’t see how we can do anything about it; he practically runs the church.”

Bill lowered his head enough for her to realize that he was feeling a little uncomfortable with the whole subject.

“Look, I don’t mean to sound accusatory or anything,” Lila said. “I was just wondering if you were getting the same vibes as me. And since you’ve been at the church longer, maybe you can help me understand if what I am feeling is totally out of character for the bishop.”

“I just get an uncomfortable feeling sometimes. Like everybody else in our congregation, I’ve put so much hope and faith in him. I think we need find out what is really going on before we make any accusations. He’s built a good reputation, you know."

With a sarcastic tone, she said, "Oh, I'm sure. He has to keep up that good reputation too. Maybe those Armani suits are necessary. Have you noticed he's upgraded his Mercedes to the newest model? I guess he doesn't feel that he has to hide it from the people. They're the ones lavishing him with money. It's like they're worshipping *him*."

Lila noticed Bill becoming more despondent as the conversation grew more intense about Bishop Hines's motives and money finagling. She was well aware that the bishop was a role model to many people in the community, and Bill was his biggest fan.

Lila was relieved that Bill had some awareness about the bishop's tactics. She knew it was futile to continue with her questioning and, besides, she didn't want to ruin her evening with Bill.

The next Sunday at church, Bill didn't assist the bishop. It was Deacon Brown's turn. Bill was standing beside Lila in one of the front pews. The services hadn't started, and everyone seemed relaxed as they waited.

A familiar figure suddenly stepped into the pew in front of them, and Lila almost gasped. The tall man had broad shoulders and a slim waist. It was Lamont. He didn't seem to notice them, but the sight of him put Lila's spirit in turmoil. Her heart started pounding, and she somehow felt guilty standing beside this white man as though they were a couple.

Lila began to battle in her head: *But aren't we? Why the trepidation?*

After the service, Lila and Lamont stood in front of the church in the brilliant morning sunshine. She had to introduce him to Bill, who was obviously with her. Although Bill shook Lamont's hand, it was clearly with hesitation. He excused himself and turned to speak to another parishioner, leaving Lila free to talk to her ex.

Lamont said, "Don't say nothing. I know you have to get on with your life. As for me, I am getting on with mine too. I'm trying, Lila. Believe it or not, I'm really trying."

Lila lowered her eyes. Lamont *was* being calm and reasonable, which was a bit of a change for him. She couldn't tell if he was high or not, but he was calm.

Humbly, he said, “I want to come by to see the kids before this week is over. Is that okay?”

“Of course,” Lila replied. “You know that’s never an issue as long as you’re sober.” A bit unnerved by the unexpected encounter with Lamont, she added, “I’m working steadily now, praise God. Have you found something, Lamont?”

“No, not really. I have been doing little odd jobs here and there.”

It was hard for Lila not to be his crutch. Normally, she would offer him a loan. However, after finishing the twelve-step anonymous program for spouses and families, she knew this wasn’t the right thing to do.

“I wanna see the kids. I miss them.”

“They miss you too. I’m afraid that before long they may forget who their daddy is—or even if they have a daddy.”

Lamont just gazed at her. When he broke off the gaze, he parted, saying over his shoulder, “See you soon, babe.”

After watching him leave, Bill joined her. “Everything okay, I hope?"

"You don't hope everything's okay and you know it."

"I beg your pardon," he said, seemingly mustering up as much seriousness as he could.

"A man pursuing a woman doesn't want to see her get back with her ex. Let's face it—that was just the standard thing to say, but it wasn't from the heart."

Bill hung his head as they walked in silence to his car. When they were in and on their way to their usual Sunday morning breakfast place, he said, "You're a lot more honest than I am."

"I didn't mean to snap at you. I know you're kind of obligated by your good manners to say something like that, even though you don't really feel that way."

The conversation over lunch was a little more serious than Lila would have liked, but the kids were busy playing with the crayons and the maze on the table. And baby Royal was asleep in the stroller.

"I believe in honesty, but I guess when it comes to what you said, you're right," Bill said. He leaned over and spoke more softly. "I do want a relationship with you, and I don't want to see your ex-husband back in your life."

"I don't think you have to worry about that."

Another silence followed, a dozen heartbeats long. He said, "Do you still have feelings for him? I know you've been through a rough time."

She took her time to think about that.

Finally, she said, "Feelings? Like romantic feelings? I don't think a woman ever forgets her first love. But, no, I don't feel particularly romantic toward him. There's been too much pain between us."

Bill seemed satisfied with that until she added, "I do pray for his recovery. I know that the pain I've suffered has been because of his addiction. I pray for him to be free of it—not necessarily for me to be back with him."

The "not necessarily" part made Bill wince ever so slightly.

# CHAPTER EIGHT

It was a bright, sunny Georgia morning, and Lila was feeling nostalgic as she drove through the quiet air. Seeing the tall green trees and feeling the fresh air hitting her face somehow made her feel uplifted.

As she left the freeway and pulled off onto a side road heading east toward Monroe, the feeling of going home filled her with joy, and the memories came flooding back. At this moment, she really missed her mom. Whenever she came home, her mom would bake her favorite dish of macaroni and cheese, and they would sit around the kitchen island and catch up on what was happening in Lila's life.

Ordinarily, she would be worried about her old car making even the short trip back home, but Bill had been maintaining it lately. Now the old car was in good shape, or at least good enough to keep her from worrying about a breakdown.

Bill had made weekend plans for them, but she used going home as an excuse not to see him. When she told him she had to go home, he offered to babysit the kids, but she didn't want to see him. It had become a routine thing, it seemed, for her to see him on the weekends. She felt confused as to what she wanted and how this had somehow become part of the norm.

This was one of the things bothering her. She knew he had been disappointed, but the need to return to her roots was overwhelming. Maybe she would learn nothing and find nothing, but she knew she needed to go home.

So she asked Desiree to mind the kids. She didn't call her dad to let him know she was coming home; she preferred seeing that gleam of surprise in his eyes when she showed up unexpectedly. Even though she felt good about going home, she was bearing a load of trouble that gnawed at her like a hungry squirrel. She had a heart full of concerns that weighed heavily on her soul—the main one being her relationship with Bill and where it was going.

He was a fine man, and *she* was the one with the problem. Were her lingering feelings about Lamont's ultimate fate causing her ambivalence? Other grappling concerns were her feelings about the bishop, about God, and about the church. It began to bother her so deeply that she simply had to get away and clear her head. She had no idea what she was going to do, but a visit with Dad was definitely overdue. She missed him.

Driving closer to the Georgia landscape of the Piedmont region, she noticed the fields were sprouting with peanuts and tobacco, and Lila thought of how it once was littered with old cotton plantations. Her heart was fluttering as she crossed the little creek just south of town, as she drove closer to home.

Other than a few cosmetic changes to older buildings and the raising of two or three more, her small hometown had remained pretty much the same. She glanced around again to find a picture frozen in time, from the cotton mill outside of town to the modest country store. However, she didn't see the small one-pump gasoline station where she used to get air for her bike tires and buy ice cream on hot summer days. In its place was a sleek new service station with a convenience store attached—the only reminder of a fast-paced and contemporary world.

She was certain her father would be home. She hoped he wouldn't be disappointed that she didn't bring the kids. He loved playing with them and telling them old stories of how she grew up, again and again, with joy.

It was Saturday, and he was always home on Saturday. One thing about her Dad was that nothing much changed in his life. His routines were sacred to him. His life was purely his ministry, his home, and fishing with boyhood friends.

She was happy to see the old Ford station wagon parked out front. With her overnight bag slung over her shoulder, she rang the doorbell. When he came to the door, he wasn't wearing his clergy garb but an old pair of sweatpants and his signature USC sweatshirt.

His face lit up at the sight of her. "Lila! What a surprise. I—"

She interrupted him as she opened the screen door. "I know, Dad. It's as much a surprise to me," she said, falling into his arms and fighting an impulse to sob. She had to control that, or else it would fill her father with concern, and that wasn't why she was here, or what she wanted.

"Where are my babies?" he asked immediately.

"They're with Des," Lila replied. "She wanted to spend some

time with them, and you know how much she enjoys them."

"I see, but so do I, honey."

Trying to escape the conversation, Lila said, "I'll plan to come back in a few weeks, and I promise I'll bring them, Dad."

"Now that makes Dad happy."

It was mid-afternoon before they finished catching up. She had all kinds of stats and stories to tell him about the kids. She avoided saying anything about her ex or Bill, keeping the conversation to family matters and home life.

For his part, nothing much had changed, except that he was excited about his plans to raise money for a new church. The old building, where Lila first learned her hymns and sung in the choir, was finally too old to be patched up any longer.

While the hometown folk, mostly farmers, weren't rich, they seemed as though they were. They were satisfied with the simpler things in life: good food, family, and a little sunshine were all they needed. There was no rat race or "keeping up with the Joneses" mentality.

When it was time to harvest the crops, everybody pitched in.

When the crops were full and bountiful in any year, they would swear they hit the lottery, and there were many thanks given to God. Everybody shared everything they had with each other, and that's just the way it was—simple and loving.

"So," Lila said, "the old church can't be repaired anymore?"

Her father was sitting in his rocker, smoking his pipe, a favorite pastime he loved even more than fishing. Most evenings would find him there, smoking and reading his Bible.

"No," he said. "The cost of a new heating system and roof alone makes it prohibitive. The land is the most valuable part of the property, so I'm proposing that we tear it down. With the grace of God, we'll build a new one in its place."

"Can the people around here afford it?"

"Well, we'll get some help from the home church, but we will just have to find a way to make it happen. I have no doubt we will do it. God always provides—always!"

Lila always marveled at his unwavering faith—one that had no room for doubt or indecision. She had to smile. "You mean with the usual fund-raisers, cake bake-offs, car washing, and all that—right, Dad?"

"That's it. The tried-and-true way, baby girl."

As they spoke, she studied the old man. He hadn't changed much. His dark hair was a little whiter, and there was another line or two around his mouth, but his eyes were as steady as ever. Those eyes were large and they slanted downward, which made him look sad. He had a full, rugged beard and his mustache was practically all white. He'd kept a close shave when Lila's mom was alive since she liked the smooth-shaven look.

Though he was a short man, he wasn't lacking in confidence. Like his faith, he was rocklike in what he thought and how he felt things were supposed to be.

While Lila had inherited, to some degree, his steadfastness, she and her sister found it difficult growing up as PKs—preacher's kids. Their status left them little room to succumb to the little temptations and sometimes mischievous ways of childhood. Rather, they always had to set the example. And while most of the time they found ways to live with it, in other ways, both girls felt that it had robbed them of some of the joys of childhood.

Lila could talk to her father in generalities, but she found it hard to get into specific issues or, worse, personal problems. She had always relied on her mother for that. It wasn't that her father wouldn't listen. It was just that she had grown up watching and listening to him preach the gospel, and to do this, as mild-mannered as he was, he had to have a certain amount of authority. She remembered that when he practiced his Sunday sermon, it was taboo to interrupt him with anything.

In some ways, her father was this perfect person, and *that's* what made things difficult. Whenever she went to him with life's issues, he would first respond by saying, "Are you still with the Lord?"

"Yes. I would never leave Him."

"Are you following His commandments?"

Dad was an old fire-and-brimstone preacher still living under the Old Testament law, which made it hard to talk with him about her imperfections.

In any case, she decided to give it a try and open up about some of her struggles of late.

As she began, there was a loud knock on the door. It was Earl Rawlins and Elroy Cummings, his fishing partners. Earl and Elroy were dressed in overalls. Earl was short and dumpy, with two patches of silver hair protruding from each side of his head and sparse strands of hair that stood up in the center. Elroy was tall and thin—less outspoken than Earl. He wore a smile with a missing tooth and no shame.

Earl said, “Is that who I think it is?”

Elroy confirmed it: “It sure is. That’s lil’ Lila.”

Lila was grinning as she let her father’s old chums in. They both had fishing gear. Lila said, “Oh, darn. I forgot. You all go fishing on Saturdays.”

Elroy grinned. “With the good Lord willing we do!”

Lila said, “I’m so sorry, Dad. You go ahead. I’ll just poke around town and spend some time with Sandi.”

Her dad looked concerned before responding. “You sure?”

“Positive. Please go ahead. I’ll be here when you get back.”

“How about I take you out for dinner when I get back? There’s a brand new steak house in town.”

"Whooie, we 'growin'," Elroy said. "Got us a new restaurant and everything."

With his big toothy grin, Earl said, "You miss the old hometown, Lila? Tired of the big city up there in Atlanta?"

Lila grinned and said, "In a way you're right, Earl." Seeing her father was still hesitant, she then shooed them all out the door.

The house was quiet, and she was now glad she was there alone. It gave her time to look around and remember. Her father kept the house the same as the day she left. There on the mantel were the family pictures. She smiled as she saw the one of their last family photos before her mom passed away. There was one with her and her sister on a fishing trip with their father, and other photos depicted landmark events such as birthdays, baptisms, and, of course, her wedding picture. She picked it up and gazed at it, with her eyes growing misty.

As she toured her childhood home, it seemed as if not a thing had been moved. Upstairs in her old room was the picture of Lamont in his basketball uniform, poised to shoot the ball. *Gosh, he was so young!*

Lamont was a budding basketball star by his junior year in high school and she was a cheerleader. They were too shy to talk to each other then, and her strict dad didn't allow any dating until she was seventeen. During their junior year, they started dating at a victory dance the school had given for the basketball team. They danced all night, and before her dad picked her up, Lamont sneaked a kiss. The rest was history.

She flopped down on her old bed and let her mind wander back to the days when everything was possible, when the world was bright and shining, and the future was limitless. Now all her girlhood dreams were gone. Her life was in limbo, filled with doubt, fear, and uncertainty.

She slowly slid off the bed and got on her knees. Folding her hands, she murmured, "Lord, what have I done wrong? What mistakes did I make? There is so much turmoil in my life. All I ever wanted was a home and family. What did I do wrong, Lord?"

A moment later, her shoulders were heaving, and for the first time in a long time, she allowed herself to feel the weight of all she had been carrying. She cuddled up to her pillow. Her old bedroom was still comforting. It even smelled the same, particularly since her father hadn't washed the covers since her mother had passed away.

She lay in bed trying to sort through her thoughts. She found herself still restless and now yearned for someone to talk to. After a few minutes in thought, she decided to call her sister Sandi. Sandi squealed with delight when she told her she was in town. "Come on over, girl. We got some catching up to do."

Soon Lila was at Sandi's modest little bungalow. Her husband, Jason, was at work. Sandi couldn't wait for her to come up the walkway, but rushed to greet her with a hug. "Come here, girl. Let me look at you. You're as pretty as ever. But…"

"But what?"

"You're troubled."

"How do you know that?"

"How do I always know? I'm your sister. Come on in. I got coffee."

Even though Lila and her sister were only three years apart, Sandi was a source of comfort and strength for her when their mother died. Sandi fixed two cups of coffee and placed them on a silver serving tray that their mother had given her for a wedding gift.

The two took a seat on the couch in the spacious living room and began to reminisce on their lives and all the dreams they once had. Lila's was marrying Lamont and being the proud wife of a professional athlete, and Sandi had hopes of a house full of kids. Both were disappointed at the cards they were dealt.

"You know, Lila, sometimes we aren't dealt the hand we want, but we must still count our blessings."

"Yes, I have been counting my blessings, and nowadays I'm beginning to think I'm a little too blessed." She gave her sister a cunning smile.

With a bewildered look, Sandi said, "Girl, what you got on your mind? It sounds pretty deep. I think I need to refresh our coffee." Sandi walked over to the stove.

"I'm seeing someone," Lila said out of nowhere.

"Yeah?" Sandi beamed. "And how's that going?"

"Well, he's a great guy. He helps me with the kids, fixes my car, and he's so attentive to me."

Sandi's smile grew to a Cheshire cat grin. "How about…you know," she said with an expectant expression.

Lila said, "Look, Sandi, I know we used to tell each other everything when we were kids, but I'm not about to tell you that." She emphasized the last word.

"Come on, Lila, give it up."

"Well, there's nothing to tell. We're not into that yet."

Sandi said, "That sounds weird. What brother would do all this for a woman and not be into…*that*?"

Lila hesitated. Then she locked eyes with Sandi. "He's not a brother."

Her sister's jaw dropped.

"He's white. His name is Bill, and he's a deacon at my church."

"Okay, now that we're over that—why not? Isn't he attractive to you?"

"It's not that."

"Then what is…? Oh, wait a minute. Don't tell me. You're

still carrying a torch for Lamont."

"No. I don't think so. No. It's not that."

"You sure?"

"No, Sandi, I'm not sure. I'm not sure of anything these days. I've got a head full of doubts about Bill, Lamont, and about church. Damn, about everything!" she said, letting it out in a torrent of frustration.

They had been sitting on the sofa, and Sandi moved closer and hugged her. "Darn it, girl! I can see you being confused about men. Shoot, who of us understands men? But the church? You've been a rock about that."

"Yeah, well. My church in the big city is different from the one we grew up in. The real word is commercial."

"How so?"

"Everything is about money."

"Well, God's church needs money to operate. You know that."

"No. It's way beyond that." Lila shook her head. "Dad wants to build a new church since the one he has is falling apart. He feels the parishioners should have a safe, comfortable place to worship God—and have room enough for newcomers so he can help them come to Christ. But in the city, it seems that the more members one has the more money it means for the bishop. It's just a lot different, I tell you…a lot different."

Sandi seemed puzzled.

Lila described Bishop Hines and then went on to share her concerns about what had been going on at the church. She didn't realize that the picture she was painting didn't show the bishop in the best light.

"That guy don't sound like no man of God. He sounds like a movie star."

Lila couldn't help but laugh at her sister's choice of words. "Well, in some ways, he *is* a celebrity," she said. "He writes books, drives a fancy car. All the women love him…and there are rumors."

"Aha. You've been missing that good old-time religion. That's your problem!"

Lila thought about that. Making eye contact with her sister, she said, “You know what, Sandi? I think you’ve nailed it.”

“About the church,” Sandi said knowingly. “What about the problem with the men?”

“I don’t know. Maybe when or if Bill and I get closer, I’ll be able to make some better decisions.”

The time seemed to slip away as Lila basked in the company of her sister. On her drive back to her dad’s house, Lila realized she didn’t get a thunderbolt revelation, but she was grateful for her big sister’s insight. She knew her, and she had enlightened her somewhat. Maybe it didn’t exactly offer a solution, but at least she better understood what she was missing in her relationship with God. She had always been close to God, always talked to Him.

However, lately she didn’t have that same feeling. It felt as if Jesus wasn’t listening as He used to. And she needed Him to listen to all her problems. Why didn’t He listen anymore? Was it something in her that was lacking? Was it that she wasn’t listening to God? Well, at least now she had something solid to think about. She hadn’t realized how much she’d missed her sister.

Lila’s dad returned from his fishing trip all happy and spry. He was proud of the two fish he'd caught. Among the three of them, they had caught five fish and, for them, that was plenty. Elroy and Earl were all smiles when they left the driveway.

Lila laughed secretly to herself as they left, thinking of the story of Jesus feeding the multitude of people in Galilee with five barley loaves and two fish. Somehow, knowing this gave her inner peace and strength.

Her father changed his clothes, and they headed out to the new steak restaurant. At one point, he said, "What is it, child? You've been my baby girl long enough for me to know when something is troubling you."

She lowered her eyes and said, "Dad, my life is unhappy, but I can't say exactly why. Nothing more has happened to me than has happened to others. And most times, I think I'm coping. But I don't feel that is true anymore. I'm feeling more and more…"

"Lost?"

"Yes."

He gazed at her, making eye contact, and then reached over and took her hand. "Then it seems, child, that I can't help you. Not today anyway." Lila knew that it was his way of making her depend on her faith more—and less on him.

Lila said, "I didn't come here to whine to you, Dad. I…I just felt I needed to come."

"And you've done right, Lila. I'm always here for you, whether we can figure out the problem or not. Love is its own problem-solver. Love can sometimes do the miracle that needs doing."

When she went to bed, she felt better. Not that anything had been solved for her. She was still in turmoil and disappointed with the course her life was taking. Bill was a fine man and was certainly doing right by her and the kids. They just didn't connect emotionally like she and Lamont had, and he wasn't what she envisioned for herself. She wondered how something could seem so right but be so confusing.

That night her dreams were so troubling that she woke up in a sweat. She prayed to God for peace and some light in her life. By the time she got back to sleep, the pink dawn was flushing over the quiet street and the birds began chirping. It was enough to lull her to sleep, but she knew that she had to get an early start to prepare for church.

She woke up early Sunday morning and fixed them both breakfast just as her mom used to do. She made his favorite breakfast: fried eggs, grits, and bacon. Since her mom passed away, he rarely got a hot breakfast. He was not much of a cook and would keep it simple to toast, juice, and some fruit. His church members always made sure he got a hot meal for dinner. She fixed him his usual hot cup of lemon tea, which he said helped soothe his throat before he delivered his sermon.

In church, she nodded and smiled at several old friends and neighbors who seemed genuinely glad to see her. She sat in her customary place up front. Sandi and Jason walked in and gave her a hug as they took their seats with the choir. Sandi was so faithful to Dad's ministry, and Lila felt she had somewhat deserted him when she had moved to Atlanta. Before she and Lamont split up, she sent offerings and supported church events as often as she could.

Dad gave a sermon that was customary for him. It was long on metaphor and allegory, and the choir sang hymns of praise. He felt that the joy of glorifying God was enough to raise people's spirits and lessen their burdens.

Lila went back in time and got right back into the spirit of the singing, marveling how the people became so emotionally involved. Sometimes she saw a tear in an eye, and other times the eyes were closed in a unique kind of rapture known only to some.

Then her dad made his appeal for the new church. It was straightforward and simple. He spoke softly yet confidently, saying, "The Lord needs his people to come together and rebuild God's temple." He explained to the congregation that they would be glorifying Jesus, and helping others to have a place to worship and learn more about God.

There was no demagoguery in his sermon, no grandiose affectations, or posturing. It was more like a father talking to his children and explaining what had to be done and why.

He gazed down at his flock and said, "How often do we get to do something so grand for Jesus? Jesus, who has done so much for us by paying the ultimate price for our sins. He has promised to bear our burdens; He promised us salvation; He promised to never leave or forsake us."

He ended the sermon with, "If anybody here believes that he can't afford to do this for the Lord, he is exempt. His brothers and sisters will understand, but we ask that you help with your prayers and give your time to make certain we do raise the money and build this new temple for the Lord, in His honor and in His glory. Amen."

By late afternoon, Lila had visited with those she had promised to see, and she was ready to go. Her father walked her to the car. He hugged her, something he rarely did, —and said, "Child, whatever is troubling you, pray. The Lord will help you. I'm sorry that I could not this time. But I will help with my prayers for you."

She hugged him back and got into the car before the tears came.

On the drive home, she did have a revelation. Why did she feel better after her father's sermon than she did after the bishop's? Was it simply because he was her dad and she loved him? No, that wasn't it. What was it?

Of course, the bishop was much more flamboyant and much more demonstrative. And that was okay. That was his style, and as long as he got through to his flock, it was okay. But it seemed his message wasn't getting through to her. Did others feel the same? She doubted it, given his popularity and downright adoration by many. What was it about her?

As she pulled up to her house, she was more puzzled than ever. One thing was for sure: she had reconnected with God's love through her father's sermon—something she had almost forgotten about since the bishop didn't mention God's love but the money the parishioners need to give.

# CHAPTER NINE

The trip back enlightened some things but turned others grayer. The slow, easy cadence of rural Georgia had lulled her back and set the pace for her trip down Memory Lane. While it brought her back to her roots and the things that had given her contentment in her earlier life, her love life was still a quandary. She tried to remember what it was that had drawn her to Lamont. Did Bill have any of those same qualities?

*How foolish*, she thought. Everybody was different. Even she herself was different by now, changed by life and circumstance. She was no longer the naive country girl who married her basketball hero. Or was she? No. Time and life had changed her. She couldn't hope to duplicate Lamont in another man. Did she still have feelings for Lamont? Would her feelings ever fade? Or disappear? How could they? Every time she looked at Royal's face, she saw him. Was she doomed to long for him her whole life?

While she had, on the surface, resisted her girlfriend Desiree's suggestions about dating and about letting her hair down, she had to admit that it was lonely out there fighting the world as a single woman, and Bill was a comfort in so many ways.

By the time she pulled up in her driveway beside Desiree's Volvo, she was tired and hoped the kids were in bed. She didn't have the energy to play or answer a million questions. She asked her friend, "Any problems?"

"Shoot, no. They never give their favorite auntie no trouble. That Royal, he's gonna be a heartbreaker, and thank God I didn't have to wash any bottles."

"Well, you can thank him for working through your Auntie Nona; she was the one who weaned him off that bottle."

"So tell me—what did he charm you into doing?"

"Nothing," said Desiree, smiling suspiciously. He's just such a handsome little bugger."

Glancing around the living room, Lila saw a new toy near the playpen. Grinning, she said, "You're just an easy score for any male with a nice smile."

Now it was Desiree's turn to grin. "At least this smile has

gotten me a few good ones."

"A few," Lila said. "Only a few."

"Maybe so, but my batting average is getting better. And I'm enjoying life."

Lila spotted a quick flutter of the exotic girl's long eyelashes, which signaled something other than enjoyment of life. Not wanting to get into it now, she simply took Desiree's hand and said, "Thanks again, girlfriend. What would I do without you?"

"I think you be doing a lot better if you gave that *Jungle Fever* you're seeing a shot."

Lila didn't reply to that.

"You gonna give him your heart?" Desiree asked, and while giggling, she added, "Amongst other things."

Lila raised her eyebrows. "Desiree!" she admonished.

"Don't *Desiree* me. Girl, you know how you get stuck in your ways."

"What ways?" Lila asked, laughing. She was interested in her friend's perception of her. She knew there wasn't an ounce of phoniness or pretension in the girl's whole body.

Suddenly, Lila felt a vibe she wasn't proud of. She said hesitantly, "Desiree, you're my best friend."

"Yeah, so?" she asked, brows raised. "I

hope…I hope…"

"You hope what? Okay, out with it!"

"I hope you don't think that I look down on you."

Desiree looked as serious as Lila had ever seen her. When she answered, she locked eyes with her friend. "Girl, why would you look down on me? I'm the only chance you got of seeing the world straight."

Lila gave a long sigh. She knew that Desiree was joking, but not entirely. She knew that Lila had a tendency to be supermoralistic and see things in a too narrow perspective. She also knew it was the consequence of being a preacher's kid. When she and her sister were growing up, they had to endure the mockery from the other kids for being "two uptight Goody Two-shoes."

Desiree now leveled her gaze at Lila. "I know what I am and who I am. I just try to loosen you up. I'm not trying to get you to do things that would make you uncomfortable."

Lila melted and threw her arms around her friend. "I know, and I appreciate it. I don't know what I'd do without you. I'm sorry. I love you."

"Love you too, girl," she said, clearly a little embarrassed and now ready to go. "See ya later."

"See ya, girlfriend. And thanks again."

The following day, Lila was anxious to talk to Bill when she went to work. When he came in, she asked, "Did you hear what everyone is buzzing about?"

"Yeah, the bishop's birthday gift." Bill seemed deep in thought. The subject was closed to him—or so it appeared.

"What are you thinking?"

"I'm just hoping that everybody doesn't go overboard and give him something lavish," Bill replied.

"The way I hear it, they're going to give him money and let him buy his own birthday present."

"That's good. I'm sure he'll do the right thing and get something that everybody agrees is appropriate."

Lila rolled her eyes, asking rhetorically, "Since when is *our* bishop appropriate these days?"

"Yeah, I know what you mean. But we shouldn't prejudge him yet. Let's give him the benefit of the doubt and hope that he does the right thing."

The next Monday, the word was already out. The gifts evidently had been very generous, and the bishop had bought himself a summer place on a lake.

Lila wasn't surprised by Bill's grim visage the next day. He was obviously upset. "I wish he had simply thanked everybody and not let it out what he had bought," he said.

"I don't think he let it out," Lila replied, "but word did get out somehow."

"He doesn't seem upset. It doesn't seem like he wanted it to be a secret. Seems he's proud of how popular he is and is in no way hiding the generosity of his parishioners."

Lila had to chew on that for a moment. "I can see how he's proud that his people think a lot of him. But let's face it: that money could have gone in a lot of better places than a summer home. Doesn't he know there are people in the congregation on fixed incomes? Some can barely pay their heating bill in the *one* home they do have!" Lila exclaimed.

Bill sat with his head in his hand in silence, apparently thinking before speaking.

"I see what you're saying, but you know, it's kind of what goes on in corporate America. The CEO gets a huge year-end bonus, because without his leadership and brilliance, the company would not be making the money it does. It is, in a way, just good ole American capitalism at work."

Lila didn't roll her eyes, but came very close to it. "Capitalism? In religion? Come on, Bill. I think a lot of people would have trouble swallowing that."

"Remember Elmer Gantry?" Bill said.

"Yeah. The demagogue con preacher who used the saint's money to build a seaside temple?"

"That's the one."

"What about him?"

"Well, the basic premise was that religion, like everything else, requires money to keep it going, and if the CEO—in this case, our bishop—enables that to happen, then God's work goes forward. Isn't that true?"

"Yes, Bill, that concept is true, but it doesn't always happen that way when greed and one's own agenda take over," she said.

He dropped his head. "I guess you're right. It's deeper than that. Truth is, he shouldn't be keeping the riches for himself. Then he becomes just like the televangelists who raise a ton of money and flaunt their lavish lifestyles."

Lila was emotionally drained with the conversation about Bishop Hines, and Bill seemed to be as well. They went back to completing their work for the day at the bookstore, going home without mentioning the bishop again.

However, Lila could not escape her thoughts. Thinking about the bishop's birthday gift ate away at her soul. She just couldn't reconcile the size of his rewards with his contribution. Even if he tripled the congregation, she felt that the money should go to worthier causes.

She had to admit that the bishop didn't spend it all on himself.

There was the new day care center that was almost finished with construction. At the request of the bishop, there would only be a nominal fee for the moms, which enabled many to go to work—whereas with the cost of regular day care, they couldn't, especially with the low-paying jobs some of them had.

And there was the Junior League. That kept many single-parent kids off the streets, involving them in healthy activities like sports and after-school plays and such. She knew that many a kid had been kept out of jail due to this program, which the bishop often helped to staff with his own contribution of time and effort. So, it wasn't cut-and-dried.

Yet something about the whole mega church bit and church capitalism did not sit right with her.

Although she and Bill didn't always see eye to eye on matters of the church, she appreciated his presence in her life and valued his opinion. Lately she was filled with so much doubt and apprehension; she questioned everything and everyone's motives. Everything seemed more complicated in her life. Problems she never thought she would encounter all seemed to be knocking at her door at the same time.

Things never panned out just the way she thought with her life. Church was supposed to be a place where you could go to worship God and learn how to become a better Christian through reading and studying the Bible. And marriage was supposed to be forever, till death do you part.

Lila felt that she was living in some sort of new world as a foreigner, not knowing what to expect. With Bill, her life seemed more simplified. Things seemed to flow naturally, like their conversations and his being a part of the kids' lives.

Lila and Bill hadn't been out alone together since she had been back from her hometown visit. One Friday night, she was preparing to see him. She remembered how relaxing it was to be away from work and the kids. Her dates with Bill made a lot of the stress, tension, and disenchantment go away.

When the doorbell rang, she ran to get it. It was probably her aunt coming to babysit. But it was early. She hurried to the door adjusting her left earring and was surprised to find Lamont standing there.

He appeared to be sober and Lila's heart melted a bit, but she knew the routine. It typically only took him a few minutes to thrust her into disillusionment. He was usually high and, ultimately, no matter what charm he laid on her, in the end there would be some kind of con designed to get some money out of her. And she knew for what. But he seemed different tonight.

"Hi, Lamont," she said suspiciously. "It's not your visiting day. What's up?"

He went into his boyish charm and started to look uncomfortable shifting his feet, seemingly grasping for words. However, he did it in a kind of charming way that made him seem like a naughty little boy. She waited.

Finally, he said, "I'm not here for what you think."

"What do I think?" she asked, almost amused.

"I'm not high, and I'm not looking for money."

"You're not? Then what do you want?"

Before he could answer, the kids came running around the corner yelling, "Daddy, Daddy, Daddy!" They were overjoyed to see their tall statuesque father standing there brandishing a warm smile. The force of the kids jumping into his arms caused him to stagger a bit. Little Royal was left tugging at his pants to be picked up. Lila could see the love in Lamont's eyes as he hugged and kissed them with passion.

After a while of playing with the kids, Lila knew it was time to get to the bottom of why he had come unexpectedly. She told the kids to kiss their dad good-bye and explained that he'd be back to see them soon. She knew saying this would keep Latoya and Jackson from whining about their dad leaving so soon. She and Lamont escorted them back to their room and popped a movie into the DVD player.

Lila was filled with anticipation as they walked down the hall back into the living room.

"Now, why is it you're here?"

"I know this is going to sound weird, especially coming from me."

She stood patiently, with no expectations, and waited.

He said, "I just want to tell you that I miss you, and that I'm sorry for what I put you and the kids through."

"What?"

"That's right. I miss you…and I love you."

Her mouth dropped a bit, and she eyed him, looking for the con. But all she could see was sincerity. He resembled the man she first met, enthusiastically telling her about his game that day. He wasn't enthusiastic now, but at least he did seem sincere.

She said, "Lamont, you have to admit that this is kind of bizarre. You show up out of nowhere and tell me something like that."

"Well, it's true."

"Alright," she conceded. "Not that I'm doubting you, but—but why are you doing this?"

Since there was nothing about Lamont she didn't know, she knew he was laying on the charm. It was the same charm that, along with his basketball talent, got him as far as he could get before the drugs brought him down.

He said, "Well, it's just that I've been talking to your father off and on for the last few months, and yesterday we got to talking about my—our—situation."

"My father? Our situation?" Lila asked. "And?"

"And he told me that if I still loved you, I should simply come right out and say it."

She cocked her head, truly puzzled. "And you are thinking we should…what? Not get back together?"

"Why not?" he asked.

"Are you in rehab?"

"No."

"Do you have a job?"

"No, I don't."

"Do you have any prospects of a job then?"

Lamont sighed with irritation. "Look, Lila, I didn't come here for the third degree. I was feeling bad, and I wanted to let you know how I feel."

"I appreciate that, Lamont, but you can't just come over here because you're not high one night and expect everything to go back to the way it was."

"Why not?"

"Because where I am now may not be heaven, but it's much

better than the hell we were in before. I'm not going to subject the kids and myself to that again. If you do what you know you have to do, if you own up to your potential as a man, then maybe we can consider it." She paused. "But not until then."

After Lamont left, Lila replayed the conversation in her mind. She wondered: *Was I too harsh? Maybe he was sincere. Maybe he really is clean?* But her sensibility told her he wasn't. And more surprisingly, she couldn't believe she had told him she would consider getting back with him if he was clean.

By the time Bill arrived for their date, she was visibly disturbed and he spotted it immediately. "What's wrong?"

"Lamont came by."

"Did he bother you for money?"

"No, not at all. In fact, he just wanted to tell me that he loved me and missed me."

Bill remained silent, and Lila briefly wondered if she should even go there, but continued anyway.

"He said that my father told him if he still loved me, he should just come out and tell me."

"With no other conditions?"

"Evidently not." Watching his troubled reaction, she said, "You know, my father was his number one fan. He always felt that Lamont was going to do great things, only to his dismay."

"Yeah," he said flatly. "But it seems like kind of irresponsible advice." Bill's reaction surprised her, but she said nothing.

Lila chose a nice restaurant and bar for their date. It was a trendy place where young, carefree singles hung out, and Lila hoped to have a fun, romantic evening, perhaps just like them. Bill wanted to distract Lila's thoughts from Lamont's love confession.

Before they got to the restaurant, he said, "I forgot something. It'll only take me a minute." They swung by his apartment, which was on the way to the restaurant. When he parked he said, "It's kind of dark out here. I'd feel better if you came in with me."

Together they went inside. He turned on only one light, embarrassed by his barely decorated apartment. Boxes were still in the corner, filled with items he had moved from his house after the divorce. He found what he needed on a small desk in the corner of the room, which was his reading space. Trying to hurry, he grabbed the item. She glanced at it.

"New book?" she asked.

"Yeah, it's not new, though. It's really kind of dated, but I had some requests for it since the movie version has been on television."

"What is it?"

"I'll tell you when we get to the restaurant." Playfully, Lila insisted.

"Okay, it's *Splendor in the Grass*."

"I've heard of it. What does the title mean?" she asked. Lila then moved to sit on the kitchen bar stool, where she held Bill's hand while guiding him over to join her.

Without a word, Bill opened the book and read a poem from its introduction. It was heart touching and ended in the words "and we were there to find the splendor in the grass."

She gazed at him. "You read it so beautifully. Would you read it again?"

She noticed how he blushed while reading the passage again. When he finished with the words "splendor in the grass," her eyes were waiting for his to find her. They gazed at each other, lost for a moment.

Lila's heart was thumping and she wondered if Bill could hear it. Suddenly, he reached for her and pressed his lips to hers. She'd always admired that he was a perfect gentleman and had never gone further than she allowed, but she folded into his arms now, kissing him passionately with tongues swimming madly, wetly, back and forth.

He slowly unbuttoned her blouse. Still locked in the gaze, he lifted her from the bar stool, and they both melted onto the plush carpet. His eyes never left hers until she unhooked her bra. Then his glistening eyes dropped and drank her in, his eyes now lustfully exploring her beautiful curves as the outside streetlights danced through the windows like silvery moonlight. Minutes later, they were making passionate love. Her feeling of lust was limitless, and soon reeling senses and sounds of passion streamed through the room.

Something about the spontaneity made the coupling so explosive. Lila had thought about this romantic evening, wondering when it might happen, but never had she ever expected such an impulsive, instinctive introduction to love.

It was as though her passion had finally crested the dam and overflowed, helpless against the flow of it, unable to struggle in the stream of it, but only able to go with it and let it take her where it may. And that was to a climax so shattering that it left her breathless.

At the restaurant, they mellowed and simply sat amid the noise and excitement, staring at each other, lost in their own little world. After their unforgettable evening was over, Lila realized that their lovemaking had not been simple lust. However, there was something about the poignancy of the poem, coupled with that look in his eyes, which triggered her own simmering need.

Whatever it was, Lila knew that their relationship had reached a new dimension and the stakes were now higher. There was no illusion that things would ever be the same.

# CHAPTER TEN

Making love had definitely changed things. Lila felt profoundly different as a result of their intimacy, but her feelings were still ambivalent. She felt closer to Bill; however, she was not operating within the comfort zone of a woman with a contented heart and sure emotions. She somehow sensed he felt the same too.

The feedback from Desiree wasn't exactly what she had expected either. Des had popped in to say hi. When Lila told her about her evening with Bill, she had expected overwhelming approval, but what she got was something completely different. And it truly surprised her.

Desiree didn't launch into any kind of backslapping, high-fiving "you go, girl" antics. Instead, she became somewhat quiet and introspective. It caught Lila by surprise, and she remarked, "I thought you were all for sex, recreational or otherwise."

Desiree smiled, but it wasn't her usual mile-wide smile, full of uninhibited fun. Rather, it was a sad Mona Lisa kind of smile.

Lila said, “What? What is it, girl?”

“I dunno,” she said vacantly. “I just hope you done the right thing.”

Lila gazed at her friend. “What? This coming from you, the ultimate party girl—the love ’em and leave ’em girl?”

“Yeah, that’s coming from me, the ultimate party girl.”

Lila gazed at her, trying to understand. Eventually, she said, “Des?” It took a moment to get the girl’s attention. “Have you had some kind of…uh…epiphany, as we say in Bible class?”

“If that there ‘efifany’ is about looking deep into yourself, then, yeah, that’s what I got.”

Lila said, “Look, I just made a pot of tea—your favorite. Want a cup?”

“If you gonna do some snooping, I’ll skip the tea.”

“I promise—no probing.”

What Lila hadn’t promised was that she wouldn’t draw out in a perfectly innocent way whatever was bothering her flamboyant friend. And that she did.

Des was telling her, “I been doin’ all this party girl stuff for a reason."

"Yeah, I know. It's called having fun."

"Yeah, that too," Des replied. "You know man and woman don't live by…what is it?"

"By bread alone," Lila filled in. "What does that have to do with your partying?"

Desiree pulled on a loose curl dangling over her cheek. "I've been doin' it, so I wouldn't remember."

Lila let that sink in. Then softly she took her friend's hand. "Remember about your little boy?"

Des sniffed. "Yeah, that's it. You read me so well, girl. And you promised."

"I only promised not to probe. And as far as I can tell, I didn't. You wanted to tell me, and you did. And I want you to know I understand."

"So you don't just think I'm some wild-assed ho?"

"I never thought that. And even if you were, I'd still love you anyhow," Lila said, adding some humor.

With that, Des began sobbing and laughing in Lila's arms.

After the crying subsided, Desiree remarked, "About you and *Jungle Fever* guy, I just hope you doin' it for the right reasons."

"And those would be?"

"Cause you love the guy. Or maybe just dig him. I know you, girl. You looking for love. Like the song says, I've been 'looking for love in all the wrong places.' At least your way is healthy." Lila's heart went out to Des as she remarked, "Just want to bury myself in something so I won't think about what I done."

Lila reassured her that the decision she had made was out of love for her child, and that she did the best thing given the circumstances. Trying to give her a glimmer of hope, Lila said, "Who knows; you may see your son one day."

Desiree's eye lit up. "You think, Lila?"

"I'm learning, Desiree, that anything is possible—anything."

When Desiree left, Lila felt good about the new closeness she felt toward her best friend, but it also left her thinking more about Bill and their newfound relationship. What did she feel? Yes, lust—no doubt about that. And the affection was just part of being Lila. But was there anything else?

She concluded that it was too early to see all the aspects of a relationship that was, after all, just budding.

The upside, she soon found out, was that Bill was around more, and he was always full of plans for them. And his plans often included the kids. He took them on outings to the zoo, to the park, and even the circus. He was affectionate and took every chance he could to steal a kiss, whisper an endearment, or flirt with Lila.

One sunny afternoon in the park, they sat with a picnic basket and watched the kids frolic on the grass. Bill said, "Your kids are great."

She grinned. "Yeah, but you wouldn't think so when they aren't playing or on their best behavior."

"Yeah, but I never had any. So I can only look at it from my ideal point of view, you know?"

"That reminds me of something I've been wanting to ask you," said Lila. "I know that your wife had fertility problems, but why didn't you ever consider adopting kids?"

He thought about the question for a minute before speaking

up. "Let me turn that around for a minute. I'll answer you for sure, but first tell me why you and Lamont *had* kids."

Lila smiled. "It wasn't any big decision. We weren't like some of these modern yuppies who decided they're gonna have two-point-three kids after they get their partnership in the firm. It wasn't anything like that at all."

"Then what was it?"

She had to do some more thinking. "You know, I never thought much about it, but I guess we were just in love and doing what people in love do. We never thought about kids, or how many to have, or any kind of sane planning about having them."

Bill seemed to chew on that for a minute. "Oh, yeah. I owe you an answer, don't I?"

"Yeah, you do."

By the look on his face, Lila could tell that the answer was coming straight from Bill's heart when he spoke.

"Maybe it was selfish of us not to adopt," he said. "I don't know. All I know is that we prayed long and hard. God gave us an answer…but it wasn't the answer we wanted to hear. It caused a lot of tension between us, and to tell you the truth, it played a big role in driving us apart."

Lila put a comforting hand on his shoulder because she could see that it was difficult for him to continue.

"We'd been together since high school," he explained, "and we'd always talked about what a great future we'd have raising a house full of kids. Of course, it never happened. I guess life doesn't always work out the way you expect it to."

"Yeah, like my situation," Lila said. The little conversation showed her another side of him, and while her own situation was different from his, she could understand his feelings.

There were more intimate evenings for just the two of them at his new place. Bill cooked her dinner more than once, and he had proven that what he didn't know about gourmet cuisine he'd taken the trouble to learn after subtly finding out what she liked.

She mentioned to him that she loved shrimp, so he undertook a rather difficult dish for a beginner: shrimp jambalaya, Cajun style. He was careful not to make it too spicy, even leaving it a bit bland. She knew he spiced it just right for her palate. She was touched by his consideration and suspected that this had to be the sweetest gesture any man had ever made for her.

And she couldn't help but fall in love with Bill—at least a little. That one incredible time they had actually made love played with her emotions every time she thought about it, and that entire evening was now forever etched into her heart and mind.

But then, there was Lamont. He never left the picture—especially when he began showing up at Sunday services regularly. She knew that Bill noticed, even though he tried to remain neutral and nonchalant about it.

At altar call, when Lamont rededicated his life to Christ, Lila tried to hide the satisfaction in her demeanor, but she couldn't. It was emotionally uplifting to see Lamont do this, even though she was in no way prepared to read any more into it regarding their wrecked marriage.

*I guess the conversations he's been having with my dad over the past few months really were helping him,* Lila thought.

Bill seemed to notice their brief exchanges during times like the rededication, but he never mentioned it. Of course, Lamont had some joyous reunions with his kids outside the church, and Bill avoided that too.

One morning at work, Bill asked Lila, "What did you think of Lamont's rededication?"

"It does my heart good to see anybody rededicate," she replied.

"And how about Lamont?"

"Especially Lamont. God knows that man needs something in his life to remind him of who he used to be and who he should be again."

She could sense what Bill was feeling, and she felt bad bringing him any discomfort. "Babe," she said, taking his hand. "You don't have to worry about Lamont because he's finally doing some things right. This doesn't mean I'm getting back with him. I hope, for his sake, that he does right, but I consider Lamont the *past*."

"You're sure?" Bill asked.

"Yeah, I am." Eager to change the conversation, she said, "Now, what's this I hear about the bishop calling a meeting?"

"He's heard some nasty rumors circulating about him, and I guess he wants us to hear his side."

"Yeah, that would be interesting," Lila said. "When is the meeting?"

"It's tonight 7:30. And I guess we're low enough on the totem pole to be invited."

"What do you mean?"

"Well, it seems he only wants us low-level types, not anybody high up in the church."

"Why do you think that's so?"

"I don't want to speculate, but I think he's just like a politician who is feeling the criticism and only wants to play to hometown or friendly crowds," Bill said. "You know, he's avoiding taking any serious fire."

"You think so?"

"Maybe I'm just turning into a cynic. I shouldn't. Let's wait and see what comes up at the meeting."

The bishop was at his most charming that evening. When he had the group's attention, he stood before them and said, "I know there have been some unsettling rumors going around, about me and about *our* success. And you know why that happens?"

He was working them just the way he did his congregation at Sunday services, asking questions like a lawyer—questions he had answers ready for.

"That happens, my friends, when one has success," he said, clearly gripping them with his powerful rhetoric. "Success is a blessing to some but a cause for alarm and jealousy to others. The Lord's blessings should never be cause for jealousy. That's the devil's domain. He wants us to turn on each other and foster these doubts and suspicions. He's the one who wants to destroy that success. Why? Because he wants you to fall astray, stop believing, and join him. Satan wants us to sink into sin and ultimate hell. That's why."

Later, he hugged each one of them as they filed out of the meeting. To Lila, he whispered into her ear, "Stay on my side, darling. You won't regret it."

As they were walking out to of the sanctuary to their cars, Bill asked, "What do you think?"

"I think he gave a great talk."

"Anything else?"

"Yeah, it was inspirational, as usual. It was uplifting, as usual and it was effective, as usual…."

"Yes?"

"But he, like our politicians, never got specific about anything. He never answered any of the questions that are fueling the rumors. Like his most recent purchases, or his book deals. No, he spoke for over an hour, had our attention, got to us, but he never really said anything."

Bill smiled. "You're getting awfully cynical there, preacher's kid. Awfully cynical."

Although she had a chuckle over it, Lila was serious about her belief in the church and its operations, and she wasn't going to sit idly by much longer if the bishop didn't come up with explanations for some of his 'big money spending.'

# CHAPTER ELEVEN

Lila now had the key to a new world and a new life—someone who not only cared but also reopened the world of love and hope with the lure of a future together. She had almost forgotten what that felt like. While it was exciting and put a bounce in her step, the thought of Lamont and his recovery still loomed in the back of her mind.

For the moment, at least, her ex might not be such a lost cause. While he hadn't rehabilitated himself, he might be on the road to a spiritual makeover. And how did that bode for her?

At this point, it was still hard to have any faith in Lamont, yet his new attitude was perplexing. He continued to be amicable with her during visits with the kids and to give her money without drama or struggle. However, Lila was determined to not fall gullible to this behavior. She had seen it before when he tried getting clean. She'd attended a drug addiction class for spouses once before when they had termed this the "honeymoon" or the most dangerous phase. It's when drug addicts act as if all is well and they've kicked the habit.

*No way am I falling for this again. I should know better*, she thought to herself.

Lila was content to enjoy her new romance and hoped that things would sort themselves out. Even going to work was an exciting adventure. Whenever she and Bill were alone in the storeroom or his office, he would insist on stealing a kiss. While Lila wasn't a starry-eyed schoolgirl and she feigned scolding him and resisting, she did like the rush of excitement in those stolen kisses. She also liked the feeling of being wanted, sought after, and appreciated. It made life worth living, and for now, at least, she was enjoying it.

Lila arrived at work one day to find Bill seemingly unhappy. He didn't scoop her up in his arms on sight, nor call her beautiful like he usually did, and she could sense something.

"What's wrong?" she inquired.

"Well…"

A customer walked toward the cash register and Lila had to wait for an answer. It was Mrs. Worthings, who usually loved to chat about books forever. Lila couldn't have been more eager for her to leave, but she was only beginning.

"What do you think about this new book the bishop is asking us to buy?" she asked while plucking the book down on the counter.

Lila replied, "I think it's wonderful, Mrs. Worthings. I hope you like it."

"Yes, but what do you think about the whole idea of it?"

Lila was writhing inside with impatience. "I think it's perfectly sound."

"Of course, the bishop wouldn't recommend it if it wasn't. So, what do you—"

Bill saw her distressed and asked, "Lila, could I see you in my office when you're done?"

Lila shrugged at Mrs. Worthings, handed her the change, and turned to head to the office. However, the old woman was obviously displeased and wanted to talk more.

Once in the office Lila turned to Bill. "Now what's up?"

"I just had a visit from a couple of gentlemen who were asking questions about the bishop."

"Questions? What sort of questions?"

"It has to do with that real estate deal the bishop talked those downtown businessmen into."

"You mean the one he's suggesting that parishioners invest in?"

"That's the one."

"I don't like it. Never did. What happened?" she asked in a convicting manner.

"Yeah, well, something's going on, and they're asking for the bishop."

"What did the bishop have to say about it?"

"I can't find him. His secretary says she doesn't know where he is either."

Cocking her head, Lila asked, "That's unusual, isn't it?"

"Yeah, Sheri is tight with him. She usually knows where he is at all times."

"What makes you think it's trouble?"

Bill lowered his voice, even as he kept an eye on the front of the store through the glass of his office window. "I think I know fire in a man's eye when I see it."

"What could it possibly be?"

"Well…you know Bishop Hines is ambitious." Bill then bowed his head. "My God…this is so awful."

"What?" she asked, inquisitively.

"It's awful enough to be suspicious of the bishop's walk. He's such a good man. He doesn't deserve our judgment."

Lila put her hand up to stop him. "Bill, with all due respect, you're like everybody else."

Lila was sensing a comedown, and her temperature was rising by this time.

"What do you mean by that?" he asked.

"What I mean is that you're mesmerized by him, like everybody else, and think he can do no wrong."

"That's not true, Lila."

"Why not? You've seen firsthand some of the financial shenanigans he pulls."

"You mean like the book sales and lavish habits?"

Lila felt bad about putting him down and took his hands. "Babe, you're trusting and you mean well. I didn't mean to say you're naive, but you've got to admit that the bishop might be up to something shady."

Sounding less defensive now, he said, "Yeah, I know. You're right." He hesitated and lowered his eyes glumly.

"I'm not saying he's all bad. He helped me get this job at the bookstore. But money does strange things to people. It corrupts them."

"I know," he said sadly. "I hope he's not in some kind of trouble. He means so much to the people of this church. They would be devastated to learn that he's anything else but a good "undershepherd."

"You're right there. He'll let a lot of people down."

Now it was her turn to hesitate. "But we should give him the benefit of the doubt. We don't know anything yet. We don't know what's happened. So, I say let's just pray for him and hope that he doesn't let us down."

"Amen, sister. Amen.

That turned out to be wishful thinking at best. A story appeared in the local paper a few days later, suggesting that the bishop was involved in some kind of scheme to defraud two big mortgage lenders.

Lila was disconsolate when she came into work the day after the article was published. “Well, Bill, seems like our prayers haven’t been answered. The bishop is up to something,” she sobbed, throwing herself into his arms, genuinely dejected.

Bill’s attitude was still one of hope. He said, “I think we owe it to the bishop to stand by him until we see how this plays out.”

“You think we should?”

“Yeah, I do. Let’s give him the benefit of the doubt.”

“You’re right,” she said, feeling a little better.

One of the things that clearly changed with Lila these days was that no matter what went wrong, she always had her relationship with Bill to fall back on. There was always something to look forward to. So, she buried her remorse about the bishop and looked forward to the weekend.

On Saturday afternoon, Lila and Bill took the kids to the park.

They spent the afternoon playing with Frisbees and footballs, sharing a picnic, and swimming.

That night after the kids were asleep, Bill announced, “I’ve got something special.” He produced a DVD.

“What is it?”

“It’s a surprise,” he said, holding it behind his back with a conspiratorial smirk.

They ordered a pizza, and Lila made some fresh lemonade.

He put the movie on, and they were happily munching pizza and drinking lemonade when she saw that the stars were Natalie Wood and Warren Beatty.

She said, “This is an awfully old movie, isn’t it?”

“Yeah, but I think you’ll like it.”

Lila gazed at the screen as Natalie Wood finished reciting the poem “Splendor in the Grass.” She turned to kiss him, realizing the sweetness of his romantic gesture of renting the movie that contained the poem that had ignited their passion initially.

Bill returned the kiss passionately, and they were getting even more into it when suddenly there was a knock on the door. Lila and

Bill exchanged a puzzled glance before Lila walked to the window. Turning around she said, “It’s Lamont.”

“What does he want?” Bill asked with an aggravated tone.

“I don’t know, babe, but I don’t need a scene. I can’t tell him he can’t come in; he’ll think something’s wrong. Please just go into the bedroom for now. I’ll get rid of him.”

She answered the door to find Lamont clearly perturbed. “What took so long? Is everything okay?”

“Yeah, everything’s okay,” she said, trying to hide her angst with a neutral tone. “I was in the shower. What is it?”

“I just had a real urge to see you. I told you I’ve been feeling that way lately.”

“Lamont,” she whined. “It’s late. Can we talk about this some other time?”

Lamont seemed suspicious and kept peeking into the living room. He said, “I just want to talk.”

She had no choice but to let him in. His eyes panned the room and immediately settled on the pizza box and the empty glasses on the table, but he said nothing for a moment. Then, “I didn’t know you had company. Or I wouldn't have come over."

"You didn't see a car in the driveway?"

"Uh, I didn't notice."

Lila saw that same spark of anger in his eyes that she remembered from the past. "I told you it wasn't a good time."

"Yeah, I can see that," he said, the anger flushing his face now. He stormed out, and Lila sat down on the couch and let out a long sigh. That's how Bill found her when he emerged from his hiding place in the bedroom. She was deflated and definitely in a different mood than she had been in earlier.

Bill now appeared to be in a foul mood as well. "Who does he think he is, coming around this time of night 'just to talk'?" he mimicked.

Lila was silent, but Bill was still fuming and making remarks under his breath that weren't as far under as he thought.

"For heaven's sake, Bill! He is the kids' daddy, and I guess he feels he still has rights."

"Yeah, and in his own selfish way he completely ignores your rights. You have a right to a life too. Believe me. He hasn't been a monk since he's been gone."

In a monotone voice Lila said, "Yeah, you got that right."

The evening ended on a sour note, but Lila promised to talk to Lamont and tell him to call before coming over so there wouldn't be another evening like this one. And she would warn him not to expect her to be free to talk to him at his own convenience.

After Bill left, Lila phoned Desiree and told her about the evening's events. She was feeling guilty and knew that Des would side with her.

She wasn't wrong. Desiree not only went off on Lamont but had some words about Bill as well.

"Your *Jungle Fever* 'gotta understand that it wasn't your fault. No need to get ticked off at you. Besides, Lila, it's time that you got in the driver's seat. Don't let no man make you feel bad 'bout nothing.' And that goes for Mr. Bill *and* that prima donna, Lamont, okay?"

After she hung up, Lila realized that Desiree was right. Things weren't the way she wanted them to be. She had to make some decisions—decisions that she had been avoiding until now.

Bill's face told the story the next morning at work. She thought that perhaps he was still miffed about Saturday night, but it wasn't that. She looked at him with shock and asked, "What?"

"We're being audited."

"By whom?"

"The church's board of trustees."

"Uh-huh," she murmured.

"Yeah, 'uh-huh' is right," Bill replied. " I don't know how to explain the bishop's book sales. I'll have to suggest that they meet with Bishop Hines if they have questions about receipts."

"We just need to turn over *all* the receipts," Lila suggested. "We need to tell them everything we know," she continued.

"I do believe that's what we have to do."

"Just how does he handle his book sales, anyway? I never understood that."

"I have an idea."

She leveled her gaze at him. "Tell me what you do know."

"It's got something to do with the number of sales, the number of complimentary copies, and the number of discounted copies.

Whatever he's doing, it's got something to do with one or all of the above. But that doesn't worry me as much as what triggered this audit by the board."

"The newspaper story?"

"Yes, and other nasty rumors going around."

"There's more?"

"There usually is in things like this."

"So what do you know about the rumors?" Lila asked."

"Only that the bishop is coming off as a money-grubber and is spending money on lavish suits, cars, and jewelry."

"I have a bad feeling about this," she warned.

"Me too, babe. Me too."

# CHAPTER TWELVE

By planning events with the kids and creating intimate moments, Bill was trying hard to impress and convince Lila that he was the man for her. He no longer pressed her to continue their sexual relationship, which was the downside of things as far as Lila was concerned. She had her reason, and it had nothing to do with not enjoying Bill's lovemaking.

The downside was that he was becoming more insistent that he, Lila, and the kids operate as a family. Lila found it hard to thwart this idea in any way, but she wasn't ready for it—at least not to the extent that Bill took it.

He was always around her house these days. She didn't want to hurt his feelings, but she didn't appreciate him always coming over without calling first. He would just pop up whenever he wanted. Lila had become a more private person while learning how to live as a single mom, and she now truly appreciated her privacy. This made it hard to live with his feel-free-to-come-over-anytime attitude.

Bill made sure they went to church together. He arranged picnics in the park, complete with kite flying and Frisbee throwing and anything else the kids seemed to like. He took them to family-type events like the circus or a ball game whenever the opportunity arose. He also took them out to dinner often, and when they ate at home, he was usually there. The only thing he didn't do was the thing that would truly consummate their relationship: live with Lila.

At work, Bill was overly attentive, taking her to lunch frequently and to after-work places on Friday nights. He wasn't openly affectionate—he never was—but whenever he had her alone in the stockroom, he would kiss her passionately.

When Lamont happened to come by, he was no longer neutral, but often openly hostile. Lila always felt her stomach churn with anxiety when the two of them were in the same room.

One Friday afternoon the bishop showed up at the bookstore with a camera crew from a network affiliate in tow. When Lila glanced up from her work, he was standing there smiling at her.

"Good afternoon, Miss Lila. Let me introduce you to my production manager, Charles Cooper."

"Good afternoon, Bishop. What's happening?"

"We're shooting a documentary as a prelude to my upcoming TV show. We want to show a day in the life of True Faith Christian Church. This afternoon's segment is going to be on life at the bookstore."

Lila cringed a bit and wondered what her hair looked like. She didn't want to primp with the camera already rolling.

Bill came out from his office, and the bishop explained to him what was going on. They were fifteen minutes into filming and Lila was ringing up sales when she turned to see Lamont approaching. Lila felt her blood pressure rise instantly. Now both men in her life, not to mention the bishop, were together in one place, and a camera was recording their every move.

Lamont walked up to Lila, who was standing with Bill behind the counter. The camera crew was now at the other end of the store interviewing a patron, old Mrs. Hubert, who was so thrilled to be on TV that she looked as if she might swallow her dentures.

Lila and Bill were sharing a light moment about Mrs. Hubert when Lamont approached them. He was looking much better these days—bright-eyed, alert, and almost like his old self.

"Hi, babe," he said to Lila. "How's my darling?"

Bill bristled at the familiar way he still talked to her. Lila was feeling the anxiety and only murmured a welcome. Bill, in a deliberate attempt to be civil and friendly, said, "How's it going, Lamont?"

Lamont, in turn, was civil but still cool. "Okay, man. How about yourself?"

Bill was about to answer when the camera crew wheeled their gear up to the trio with the bishop close behind. The commentator had a mic in his hand and a glib smile on his face; the soundman looked bored and was swinging a mic; and the lighting man toted an array of lights. Then there was the cameraman, who was trailing all kinds of wires as he tried to focus on the best shot. Overall, it was quite a production.

The show's commentator said, "Hello, folks. We're enjoying our visit to Faith Christian and the spirit of revival that's going on here, thanks to your bishop."

All three murmured and shuffled their feet, completely unprepared for an appearance on television.

"I know this is kind of an impromptu visit, but our network likes to see people when they don't know they're on the air. So, who are you fine folks?" He put the mic to Bill's face, and Bill introduced himself.

Then Lila got the mic in her face. The commentator spotted Lamont, and he stuck the mic under his nose and said, "Are you a patron, sir?"

"Well, yes, I am. But today I'm here to visit my wife."

"I see. Who is—?"

"This lady here," he said, motioning to Lila.

The TV commentator said, "Well, what a good-looking couple. There are some handsome people here at Faith Christian, folks—very handsome."

If there was a hole to crawl into, Lila would have done so. Thankfully, the crew moved on to another target of opportunity. Bill was red-faced and tight-lipped. Lila was anxious, and Lamont was grinning.

When she glared at him, he innocently said, “What? You’re not my wife? You’re not beautiful? What’s the problem?”

She knew he was gloating at how uncomfortable he had made her and especially how angry he made Bill, who stalked off to his office.

As he followed the camera crew out, the bishop turned and flashed Lila a bright smile and a thumbs-up.

“He’s a happy man. He loves this stuff,” Lamont said,

“He sure does,” Lila said in a world-weary way. “He’s a man who truly belongs in front of a camera.”

Since Lila had a moment alone with Lamont, she scolded him about his comment about her being his wife.

Pointing her finger at him, she sternly said, “To answer your questions: I’m your ex-wife; yes, I am beautiful; and you’re the problem.”

Lila could tell by the smile on Lamont’s face that he wasn’t embracing her contempt. Her words were more like music to his ears if anything.

"What's your boss so miffed about?"

"He's not miffed. He had to go. He has a lot of work to do."

"Uh-huh," Lamont said with a smirk.

She left Lamont standing there enjoying his moment of victory as she went back to Bill's office. She knew he wouldn't be working. Instead, he was sitting there sulking.

"What's the matter?" she asked innocently.

"Nothing," Bill answered, still tapping his fingers on the desk.

"Oh…nothing?" She waited, but he didn't say anything. "So you're going to be mad at me for nothing?"

"I'm not mad. I know you didn't do anything."

"I rest my case," she said with a smile, trying to inject some mirth.

"But…" he said.

"Uh-oh. Here comes the *but…*"

"You did give him a real welcoming smile."

"Bill, puh-leeze," she intoned. "I don't hate the man. He's the father of my children. Why should I give him the cold shoulder?"

"I don't expect you to give him the cold shoulder. It's just…"

"Just what?" she said impatiently.

"Well, maybe not be so warm?"

"Bill, you know how things are. I wish you wouldn't stoop to petty jealousy. I thought you were above that kind of thing."

"Yeah, well, maybe you give me too much credit. I only know that I want a future with you, Lila, and the only thing that could hinder that is *that* man."

She reached out and touched his arm. "Bill, you're being overly emotional about Lamont. I don't think he's any threat to us."

He looked up. "I'm sorry. But if you don't know by now how much I love you, then I've done a bad job of expressing myself. I don't want to lose you."

She walked around the desk as he stood up, and in one fluid motion, she was in his arms. "You're not going to lose me, babe. I'm no ingrate. You came along when I was at my lowest point. The last thing in the world I want to do is make you unhappy."

"It isn't your gratitude that I want, Lila. I want your love."

"I didn't mean to make it sound that way. I was drowning and sinking fast. You were there for me. That's what I meant. And if it sounds like gratitude, isn't that part and parcel of love?"

"I—I guess I'm not feeling very secure about us."

"Why not?"

"Well…I—"

She interrupted. "Is it the sex thing?"

"Well, no…I…"

"Sure it is. I thought I had explained that to you."

"You did, but living the celibate life after having…you know…"

"Yes, I know," she said, her tone softening. "I know exactly what you mean. It was wonderful for me too, and that's exactly why I want to do things right. We both have to be sure that we have a firm relationship going before we get off track in a sexual relationship that will have a life of its own. I want it to all be part of God's plan for us."

He dropped his head. "You make a lot of sense, Lila. If he hadn't showed up today, I wouldn't be like this."

"I know, babe. I know. All I can ask is that you be a little more patient so we can both see how this all shakes out."

# CHAPTER THIRTEEN

Lila phoned her dad every two weeks to check on him and make sure he was in good health. After they caught up on what had been happening with other family members, the community folks, and the church, her dad asked, “Did Lamont tell you that I helped him get a job with the city athletic department?”

“No, Dad, but I’m glad to hear it.”

“I hope that boy will do the right thing now.”

Lila’s hesitance did not escape him, for he responded, “You have doubts?”

She sighed. “He’s done this in the past, Dad. He’s given me and the kids much needed money before. But like I said, I’ve seen his good behavior before and it usually doesn’t last long.”

“Don’t be pessimistic, Princess. He’s going through a real tough thing. I do addiction counseling, and you probably have no idea how difficult it is.”

“I don’t mean to sound down on him, but I’ve been there before. In the past, whenever he gets his hands on some money, the kids and I see none of it."

"I understand how you feel, child, but the Lord wants us to be positive and upbeat. Nothing good can come from negative thinking. It clearly tells us in Philippians 4:8: 'We should think on things that are honest, just, and of good report.'"

With an uplifted voice, she said, "Yeah, I do know it, Dad. Maybe I can't recite it chapter and verse like you can, but I do know it."

A beeping horn ended the conversation. "Gotta go, Dad. As always, it was nice talking to you, and I know I can always count on you."

After she hung up, she thought about what her dad told her. He was the only man in her life who didn't seem to have a motive for being in it.. After another beep drew her out of her reverie, she headed for the door. It was Desiree, who was giving her a ride to work.

Des was unusually upbeat that morning.

"What's with you, girlfriend?" Lila said with a grin. "Knowing you, there's only one thing that can give you that glow in your cheeks."

"Oh, shoot, girl. You think you know everything."

"New boyfriend. Right?"

"Shut up," Des said with a big grin. "You, a Christian lady, and you can't tell the difference between real enlightenment and some new boyfriend?"

Lila returned the grin. "Yeah. Right. Enlightenment."

Des suddenly turned serious. "You don't think I'm capable of seeing Jesus's light when it shines on this sinner?"

Lila quickly realized that she wasn't kidding. "I'm sorry, Des, but I really was joking. Nobody could be happier than I am that you've found our Lord."

"It's okay, girlfriend. I can see how you would doubt ole Des being on the righteous path."

After a few seconds of silence, Lila looked at Des. With the grin back on her face, she said, "Okay, so you'll tell me about it when you're ready, right?"

"As always," Des replied.

Des had a new subject and seemed eager to discuss it. "I heard that Lamont got himself a job."

"Yeah. That's true." After a moment Lila added, "Where did you hear it?"

"The bishop told me."

"Yeah, well, I'm hoping for the best. A week doesn't go by that he doesn't buy something new for the kids. He left a new basketball for Jackson the other day, and something for the baby too. It's like the Lord is in him and he's trying to make amends. At least that's what I hope."

When Lila got home that evening, she found an envelope slipped under the door. It was a money order from Lamont. She stared at it as her mind considered the implications. Maybe Lamont was turning a corner. But time would tell.

Whatever epiphany Lamont had was working because he not only provided a check every week, but he also began stopping by to take the kids for an afternoon or a Saturday morning. When the kids returned, they were full of all kinds of stories about the fun they had with Daddy.

Since this cut into Bill's time with Lila and the kids, it began to resonate with him—and not for the better. They started getting into little squabbles about it.

Lila was beginning to lose patience with him. “But, Bill,” she said, “he’s their father. I can’t take time away from him. Surely you can see that.”

It was a reasonable argument, but he didn’t take it reasonably. Instead, he reacted in a way that was selfish and uncharacteristic of him.

After one such squabble, she took his hand and stroked it. “What is it, babe? You’re not yourself. You can’t, or you shouldn’t, feel threatened in any way because Lamont is finally living up to his parental obligations.”

“It’s not that.”

“Then what is it?”

Her question was met with silence and a lowered head. She asked again, “What is it? Do you feel that somehow there is less of a commitment from me?”

He finally spoke up. “Maybe. Perhaps something like that.”

“Well, you shouldn’t feel that way. Lamont is doing the right thing. That's not a reason for either of us to feel bad or in any way threatened."

Her comment made Bill feel remorseful, and while trying to dismiss that position and liven up again, he reminded her of the big football game they had planned for all of them on Saturday.

The kids were eagerly waiting early Saturday morning and Lila's aunt was visiting, preparing to do some back-to-school shopping before the game. Before Bill arrived, Lila had to pop out for some last-minute things. She hoped to be back before Bill arrived. But even if she wasn't, he was always happy to involve himself with the kids, so she wasn't concerned as she drove off to the supermarket.

Lamont showed up at the door while Lila was at the supermarket, taking her aunt by surprise. "Lamont, how nice to see you," she said. "I'm hearing good things about you."

"Thanks, Auntie." He wasn't shy about still calling her "Auntie" just as he always had.

She asked, "Do you like your job?"

"It's great. I get to do what I love best, and it's so good

watching these kids develop their skills. I love bringing them along. It gives me a…"

He was rambling, and it seemed to embarrass him. He stopped rather abruptly, and although Aunt Nona encouraged him to go on, the moment had passed.

Instead, he simply said, "I got some unexpected time off, and I wanted to take the kids for the morning. I hope that's okay."

Aunt Nona hesitated. "Lila is out to the store. Does she know this?"

"I didn't have time to tell her. I didn't know I was going to have this time off."

By now, the kids were clinging to Lamont's legs, yelling, "Daddy, Daddy," while clamoring for his attention.

He scooped Royal up in his arms and said, "Boy, you getting big. Soon I'm not gonna be able to lift you. You guys wanna go with Daddy?"

The uproar overwhelmed Nona, and she acquiesced. Soon they were out the door.

Lila got home a little later and was shocked to find the kids gone. When her smiling aunt told her about Lamont popping over unexpectedly, the young woman's face dropped.

"Oh, God, this is going to make Bill flip out."

Her aunt, now worried, put her hand on her throat and said, "Oh, dear, I clearly forgot about your plans to take the kids to the game. They were so excited to see Lamont that I got carried away."

"Don't worry about it, Auntie. It isn't your fault. We'll just have to find them and pick them up." She didn't add that she knew he would go ballistic when he found this out.

Her mood was ambivalent by the time Bill arrived. She knew how he was going to react, and even so, there was another emotion involved: resentment.

*Bill will have to learn how to handle disappointment better*, she thought.

"I've been planning this for how long? And he just waltzes in here and scoops the kids up. How did you let this happen, Lila?" Bill blew up. She wasn't wrong. She came close to rolling her eyes.

"I told you I wasn't here. I had to pick some things up at the store, and by the time I got home, Aunt Nona had already let him take the kids."

Bill didn't dare blame her aunt, but considering the glare in his eyes, he must have held Lila responsible. "Well," he said, "what do we do now?"

Lila stroked his arm. "No need to get all upset. We can check out the places he usually goes, like the park and the pond. I didn't check whether the kids took their toy sailboats, but maybe they're at the pond sailing them."

They set out to find Lamont and the kids, but Lila was already losing her high spirits about the game and the shopping afterward. Bill's mood didn't temper because he wouldn't let it. He somehow seemed to view the situation as a personal affront against him.

They got in the car and searched to find Lamont and the kids. As they made the rounds of the usual recreation spots, Bill's face—now fixed with a permanent scowl—seemed to darken as rage built up within him.

Searching desperately, they were surprised they didn't find

them at the usual places. Bill began to mutter, "He knows what he's doing. He won't be at the usual places!"

Lila, herself on the edge, said, "Damn it, Bill. Do you really think Lamont came over to get the kids to stop you from taking them on an outing?"

"Yeah," he snapped, "and he found out from somebody. Your father, maybe? He's been in his corner I see."

From her place in the passenger seat, Lila now folded her arms and ratcheted her head slowly toward him. "You make it sound like a plot against you. The man is trying to do the right thing, to the benefit of his kids, and you act like it's a damn conspiracy aimed directly at you."

His face reddened, and he didn't answer. After a little more cruising around, Lila suggested, "Let's try the outdoor basketball courts at the city park. He's been teaching Jackson to shoot hoops. Maybe they're there."

"Shoot hoops? That's the first I've heard of that."

Again, she turned slowly toward him. "Well, who would be in charge of telling you that? And why is it so important? Surely he can do what he wants with his own kids."

"Surely," he intoned, the sarcasm palpable.

This threw Lila into her own sulk, and the intensity went out of their search. By the time they got home to find the kids still gone, both their spirits were wrecked and neither had much enthusiasm for the football game. Lila saw a note on the table from Aunt Nona saying she would take the kids shopping tomorrow.

Worn out from the whole episode, Lila suggested to Bill that maybe he should go home. Without hesitation, Bill stood up and said, "I'll see you at work tomorrow."

Lila wasn't surprised that Bill didn't give her the usual hug before departing. Concerned over a possible confrontation, Lila was relieved to know that Bill wouldn't be there when Lamont arrived with the kids.

Lamont finally returned with the kids several hours later to find Lila fuming. The kids were still excitedly storming into the house from their outing as she began to sternly lecture: "Lamont, what did I tell you about these unannounced visits?"

Before Lamont could respond, Lila threw her hands up and

added, "Don't ever take my kids *anywhere* without telling me."

"Wait a minute. They're my kids too. Besides, I didn't think it would be a problem."

"That's not the point, and you know it."

"I'm sorry Lila. I guess I wasn't thinking. It's just that I had some free time from work and I wanted to spend it with the kids."

"Can I…"

Lamont tried. "Let me help you get them washed up for bed, okay?"

Lila looked him up and down before reluctantly complying with his request and began to thaw a bit as they prepared the kids for bed. Seeing him involved with the kids reminded her of how he was before the drugs took over his life. It was customary for Lamont to make time for the entire family, especially her.

After the kids were tucked away in bed, Lila walked Lamont to the door. With mixed emotions, she begged him, "Please don't do this again. I have a schedule for the kids and if you want to see them, call first."

"I promise I'll call from now on. I can't handle you ever being this upset with me again. Listen, I know I've hurt you and the kids before, but that's all behind us now. I want to do whatever I can to be the father and hus—"

"Good night, Lamont," Lila interrupted, while closing the door. She then sat on the couch and reflected. *Did Lamont just imply he was going to be my husband again?*

The dark cloud over Bill and Lila's relationship didn't dissipate. Nothing more was said about the missed football game.

At work there was a definite chill in the air. This made Lila wonder how solid her relationship was with this man. With the recent events, he seemed more concerned about outdoing Lamont than he was about making her happy. To make things worse, Lamont came in more often and made sure he hung around long enough for Bill to come out of his office and notice him.

He would always offer a cheerful hello to Lila's boss, which was always met with a curt and cold response.

Even after the ice melted, things between her and Bill still were not back to normal —at least not to status quo. Even if she wanted to forget the chaos about the football game, she still had doubts about building their relationship on false pretenses.

Lila knew that Bill and his ex-wife couldn't have children, and he no doubt wanted to be a father. She had assumed that's why he had been so attentive and interested in the kids.

However, these days she wondered if it wasn't more about being in competition with Lamont than anything else. After all, while Lamont was an unemployed drug addict, he was little to no competition.

What Lamont could do for Lila and the kids couldn't compare with Bill's input and contribution, for he was steady, sober, loving, and new! Further, he was mature and responsible, whereas Lamont was little more than a faded basketball hero with no future and a load of baggage. Bill had a future and Lamont had only a speckled past.

So now that Lamont was back into the competition, Bill didn't like the evening of the odds. Whatever Christian charity he had for others did not extend to Lamont, and Lila saw that as the work of the devil.

Des seemed to be around more, often stopping by the

bookstore to take Lila out to lunch. This last time Lila agreed but said, "I refuse to let you pay for lunch today. I've got some money, so it's my treat."

Des raised her eyebrows. "Whoopee. Ole Lamont's money is coming steady now?"

"Yeah, it is."

When they got back, Desiree's loud laughter brought Bill out of his office. Since Bill and Des had never met formally, Lila introduced them.

After she had gone and her loud speech and laughter had stopped reverberating in the quiet bookstore, Bill had a distasteful look on his face.

Lila stared him down. "What?"

"Nothing," he said flatly. It was the kind of 'nothing' that meant something, and Lila could only guess. Yet she didn't want to push him because she didn't think she would like what was bothering him.

Things in their relationship had turned down a few degrees from where it had been.

# CHAPTER FOURTEEN

It was Friday night—a time when Bill and Lila were usually together at Stooges having some dinner, watching a game, and enjoying each other's company in the friendly, raucous ambience. However, tonight Des was coming and for the first time ever, Bill gave a lame excuse for his absence.

Lila was actually relieved since the tension between them made her uncomfortable. She wouldn't look forward to the evening with her usual enthusiasm anyway. Besides, it was nice to be with Des and to catch up.

They arrived and found a table on the patio near the rear, away from the TV and the occasional uproar of cheers for the home team.

Des, as usual, was curious. "So where's *Jungle Fever* this evening?"

"Knock it off, Des. He had something to do."

"Uh-huh."

The response had a little uncertainty to it, so Lila rolled her eyes and said, "What—we have to go out every single Friday night?"

"No, not really," she said, "but it sure seems like things have cooled down."

"They might have," Lila said, sipping her Coke. "But I like to think that we're just going through a rough patch. Know any relationships that don't?"

After Des realized that Lila wasn't going to nibble at her bait, Lila set the agenda for the conversation. Her first question suggested to her friend that she was dropping the light mood and was getting serious. "So, Des, how close are you to accepting God as your personal savior?"

"Wow," Des said, "you know how to get to the point." Des leveled her gaze at her friend. "Ya' know, I don't mean to kid about everything. If anybody needs God in her life, it's me."

"And?"

"And I didn't know how to tell anyone, but I have a new love. God."

Lila's eyes filled with tears of joy. "Why didn't you tell me, Des?"

"I was waiting for the right time, when we got some girl time together. You always busy with the kids or doing the *Jungle Fever* thang these days. I thought I darn near had to make an appointment to see you."

The two of them shared a laugh. Then Des got serious.

"It's an amazing feeling to think that God loves you and wants you to be happy…that if you believe in Him and love Him, He will love you back. He will keep a place for you in heaven. I can't tell you, Lila; that is just *so* unbelievable for someone like me."

"What do you mean—someone like you? Haven't you learned that Jesus, our Lord, considers you as good a person as the president of the United States or the pope or the king of England?"

"Yes, I know. That's what's so hard to believe. You go through life not thinking much of yourself, and then one day it's like a light shines into your life, into your…your…I don't know, your soul, I guess. It lights you up and makes you feel so loved. You feel so loving to other people. I got to thank the bishop for what he's done to open my eyes."

"Well, yes, Des, but the bishop is only God's messenger and shepherd to lead the way for us."

"He's a lot more than that. He is 'the man,' girlfriend. I tell you, that man has the Lord in him. He walks with God."

"We all walk with God, Des. The bishop's job is to help keep us all on the right path by teaching us God's word."

"Well, to tell you the truth, Lila, I never met Jesus, or the Lord, but I have met the bishop, and for me, he's the living God. That don't take away what I feel for Jesus and the Father. It's just that without the bishop, I wouldn't really have met Jesus or had Him in my life."

Lila was startled at her friend's admission and knew she had to help Desiree put things into the right perspective. After all, this religion thing was a huge and new experience for Des —probably earth-shattering. Lila reached over the table and grasped the girl's hand. Des had tears in her eyes.

"I'm so happy for you, Des. You are seeing the light—the Lord's promise for us all."

"Thanks, babe," she said, sniffing. "Look at me, blubbering like a child."

"It's what we go to church for, Des. It's what it is all about." After taking a few moments to think, she said, "And it's what bothers me sometimes about this idea of super-religion and super evangelists."

"What about evangelists?" Des asked.

"Oh, you know. This whole idea that churches must be rich and prosperous in order to get the word out. That old-time religion is for backward country folk."

Des's eyes widened. "But I *am* backward country folk. I never tried to fool anybody about that."

"Yes, but part of what Jesus has asked us to do is spread the word, and what I'm saying is that I don't think you necessarily have to be a rich and super powerful church in order to do that."

Des sipped her drink and looked up. "So I take it that you don't like what Bishop Hines is doing with his TV show and how he's been talking about we should give more money to support his causes?"

"That's right. And I am beginning to have my doubts about the bishop too."

This appeared to shock Desiree. "What do you mean?"

"Well, I don't know how much you hear, but we in the Faith Christian work force hear a lot about things the bishop is doing and things he is alleged to be doing."

"What you talking about?"

"Look, Des, I know that you are just finding the Lord and all, but sometimes we have to worry about our shepherds."

"You talkin' about the bishop?"

"Yes. He does things that might not be completely on the up-and-up."

"You sayin' the bishop's a crook?"

"No, not really. Not in simple black-and-white terms anyway. He's not stealing, exactly, but he does seem to be doing some unscrupulous things."

"Unscrupulous?"

Lila knew she was going over Desiree's head with rhetoric. She didn't want to engage in a hypercritical conversation with her, but she still felt compelled to make her understand.

"Des, some people believe that whatever you have to do to make something good happen is worth it—even if you have to do something dishonest to make that happen. They call it 'the ends justify the means.' It's a philosophy that lots of people believe in."

"Anything like that in the good book?"

"No. It's like…well, it's like you get better things for more people by doing something that might be dishonest and hurt a few people. 'It's for the greater good' kind of thing."

Des sipped her drink, lit a cigarette, took a drag, and said, "You got any proof the bishop done something like that?"

"Kinda."

Des stared at her and waited.

"It's like what he does with his book sales. He exploits the store's facilities in order to favor his own book over other authors."

"That just sounds like business to me. No crime there. What else?"

"Well, maybe that's kind of a trivial example. But another example would be that he is having political groups with money buy up his books so he can reach best-seller status without earning it by readership."

"Say what?"

"Maybe I've simplified it, but the bottom line is that he's making money for his own purposes and not in a legitimate way."

"But don't he do it for True Faith Christian? To let him reach more people?"

"That's one of his reasons." Lila hesitated. There was more on her mind.

Finally, she said, "Look, Des, I am struggling with his ethics too. I want to believe in him, and I think he's done a lot for TrueFaith Christian and for many people. I want to believe that what he is doing is needed for the benefit the of the church and not to make himself more successful or popular in the business world. What matters to me is that there is money being made to help the people of his church, which I can believe in. So, I'm not talking against the bishop, and I'm not saying he's necessarily unethical."

She stopped a moment to let her thoughts catch up with her emotions. "I just wish I were sure that what he was doing was in the best interest of everybody."

Des was all intent on listening to her.

"And," Lila added, "not just his best interest."

Des gazed at Lila for a while. "Church is all different than when you were a kid at your daddy's church out in the country, right?"

"Yeah. Very different, and sometimes I miss it."

"Maybe the bishop's just using modern kinda stuff, like politics and all, to help the church. And ain't that what all powerful kinda folks do? I gotta admit it's all beyond my poor little brain, but that don't mean it's bad—or the bishop either, for that matter."

Desiree took another sip of her drink and said, "I thought I was the one who was the cynic around here. Now it seems that it is you who is questioning everything."

"I know you've come into something real new, Des, and you like and appreciate the bishop for helping show you the way. But God's goodness and message is the same whether any of his shepherds here on earth are corrupt or not. I hope I haven't put you off about God and being born again because of what I said about the bishop."

"I'm not put off. I still feel good about being nearer to God."

"That's great. I'd feel terrible if I thought I was the one who put a bug in your ear about church and our Lord."

Lila worried about her conversation with Des all weekend. Bill wasn't around much, and she had a lot of time to think. Des was no scholar, but she wasn't a stupid person either, and Lila hoped that she had understood what she was trying to say. It was hard enough convincing unbelievers to come to Christ, then having to share with them that not all Christians are living up to what God expects—and much worse to explain that the bishop of the church may be involved in unethical behavior.

It broke Lila's heart to have this conversation with Des. But Lila felt it was for the best, before Des succumbed to any of his whims.

A few weeks later, she was working overtime. She usually didn't work late unless Bill did, but he was still in a tiff about the football game. She wondered how much maturity he was displaying by holding a grudge for so long.

She found herself alone in the building. When she finally went out to the parking lot, she couldn't help but notice that the bishop's BMW was still there. And across the lot was another familiar car: Desiree's old Volvo.

She was about to get in her own car when she felt an urge to talk to Desiree and find out if she was all right with what they had talked about earlier. So, Lila used her key and went back into the building. She was approaching the end of the building and the administrative offices when she heard some sounds. As she got closer, she began to recognize them. They came from the bishop's office.

It was a frosty glass-partitioned office within another reception area, where his secretary sat during work hours. Desiree's body language alone suggested more than a notion of what Lila was hearing. In the end, it wasn't what Lila was hearing but what she saw that set her world tumbling. She noticed the silhouette of a man and a woman and there was no mistaking what they were doing. The noise, the passionate voices, and the knocks were the unmistakable age-old sex sounds.

Lila couldn't bear what she was hearing and seeing. She ran down the corridor in a disheveled haste. Finding her car, she simply had to sit still in it for a few minutes to gather her thoughts and to calm her pounding heart. *What a turn!*

Her first impression was that this couldn't be good for Desiree. The bishop was a married man, and Desiree was just a novitiate in the church and in the religion. This could ruin her—set her back for the rest of her life. Yet she didn't know how to handle it.

After all, Des was her best friend and most intimate confidante. If she couldn't talk to her about it, whom could she talk to? For a minute she thought of Bill, who would be her most natural and obvious ally. But right now Bill was stewing about his own issues and might not be the right person to talk to. Still, she had to talk to someone. It was eating her up.

After having spent a restless and sleepless night, she thought again about telling Bill, but her first glance at him that morning changed her mind. He was still sulking. There was no telling how he might react.

Then she got to thinking that the only person she should talk to about this was Desiree herself. However, that seemed reckless and not at all discreet. How could she explain that she just happened to see them making love in the bishop's office? Anybody would consider that spying, especially after the conversation they had had about the bishop.

She knew that Desiree was vulnerable and that the bishop was taking advantage of her. He was convincing in everything, and a new Christian-like Desiree was impressionable. She felt that the bishop was right about everything and was a man of integrity. Lila imagined that  told Desiree that he loved her, or worse still, acknowledged his desire to know her flesh.

This was a major dilemma. She couldn't approach her friend about the damage she was doing to herself and her blossoming faith without revealing that she had, in fact, spied on her. Lila was aware of Desiree's bad-girl image. Who knew how all this would affect her newfound faith? Lila wanted nothing to interfere with the jubilation of Desiree accepting Christ.

She pondered about talking to her father, but the more she thought about it the more she realized that he was too strict and old school, and therefore wouldn't understand the situation in its full context. Or would he? She feared that he would judge Desiree and take some sort of public action against Bishop Hines. There was no room for nuances or forays into modern philosophy for him. Things were either right or they were wrong.

*No, that wouldn't be a good idea*, she thought. But it was driving her crazy, and she had to talk with someone.

# CHAPTER FIFTEEN

Lila had been praying for an answer to her dilemma and it came in an odd way. Bill had thawed a bit and asked her if she would like to attend the seminar the bishop was hosting the next weekend at a resort in Hilton Head, South Carolina. It would be a chance for them to be together, learn more about their faith, and renew their personal relationship.

Lila was tempted to talk, but after some soul-searching, she realized that it wouldn't be a good idea. For one thing, she now had *bigger* questions about Bill and how he had handled the situation with Lamont and the kids. The last thing she wanted was to keep the kids from their father no matter how Bill felt. She also felt that he was trying to move their relationship too fast, and she needed some time to sort things out. For those reasons and more, she declined.

Lila agonized over the best way to confront Desiree about her affair with the bishop. Was there a best way to begin with? She had attempted several times to get Desiree alone to speak with her, but Des was always too busy with either a work or an after-work function. Lila knew that her best friend was just trying to avoid her.

It wasn't until Desiree mentioned that she was going on the trip that Lila decided to go along. She knew that this was the perfect opportunity to confront Desiree and keep them apart while at the resort, which would no doubt be a glamorous locale. Maybe she could make Des see the light and stop this affair before rumors got out about it.

In any case, the bishop wouldn't want to continue if he knew that Lila was aware of his affair with Desiree. Maybe, Lila thought, she could do it in such a way as to appear innocent. After all, Des didn't realize at this point that she knew about their affair.

As Lila registered for the conference, one of the church's officials told her that there were no more seats on the bus or rooms available at the hotel. All the attendees' names were given to the bishop and his secretary, so Lila couldn't sneak her name on the list without notice now.

Lila's wheels began to spin feverishly. Why didn't Des tell her about the limited seating? Usually they would look out for each other and make sure the other had a seat and a room. *Was this done intentionally*? She wondered. This made Lila even more adamant about going on the trip. She couldn't let on to Desiree what her true reasoning was for going on the trip: to spy on her and unleash her from the bishop's contrived love grip.

When Bill approached her about her plans for the weekend, she immediately said, "I'm going to the country to visit my father." She hated lying to him, but she felt this was the only way to have some free time to do what she needed to do to get Desiree away from the bishop.

If Bill came along, he would monopolize her time by wanting to get closer to her. When he hinted that he would like to go along, she said, "Oh, no. My father is a great guy, but he's too old-fashioned. He wouldn't understand our relationship."

Bill didn't argue, but seemed relieved that Lila talked as though their relationship was still very much alive. He had worried lately that he'd been too obstinate and was well on his way to ruining things.

The parishioners were all traveling by chartered bus. The bishop normally drove his own car, and today he rode alongside the bus to supervise rest stops and look after his flock. Lila didn't think that Des would be bold enough to travel alone with the bishop in his car.

After arranging for her Aunt Nona to mind the kids, she took off before the bus's scheduled departure time at eight in the morning. By six, she was on the road, heading north to Hilton Head, two hundred miles to the northeast traveling by the interstate.

She finally arrived at the oceanfront Marriott. It was gorgeous, and she knew she only had a short while before the True Faith Christian bus arrived. She decided to have a cold drink out on the patio to help her relax and think out her plan to get the answers she needed.

Ordering a lemonade, she sat and finally relaxed. The startling blue Atlantic stretched away to the horizon and sparkled in the sun like a million diamonds. The surf was running high, and the waves crashed ashore in a resounding tempo that was almost mesmerizing. Groups of imported coconut palm trees in the patio area and near the edge of the beach gave it a tropical ambience.

She nursed her drink and pondered her first concern, which was whether she had the fortitude to follow through with her plan. It was pretty bold, and she was, in fact, laying down the gauntlet to the bishop. How would he react?

She was fairly certain how Des would react, just as she had seen her when she felt lust before. Des became territorial and obstinate; nobody could interfere with her love. Only after she crashed and burned would she come crawling back to her friend, looking for comfort. Her best chance of a confrontation would come from Des.

Lila pulled the seminar itinerary out of her handbag and checked it out. It called for an afternoon of rest after the bus trip. That evening there would be a prayer service and a dinner. Tomorrow the religious preaching and program led by Bishop Hines would start, continuing with some prominent guest speakers who were also on the program. The seminar wasn't just a homegrown affair strictly for True Faith Christian parishioners. It was designed to bring TV coverage and publicity for Bishop Hines and his upcoming TV evangelist program.

Lila could have sat out on the beach all afternoon. Having never seen the ocean before, she was awestruck. But she would bask in its beauty later. She knew that she should get up to her room and stay out of sight so she could prepare for this evening's prayer meeting and dinner. Later that afternoon she saw the True Faith Christian bus pull inside the parking lot along with the bishop's car. Des did not alight from the BMW but came off the bus with the group.

Lila came to one conclusion that afternoon. If she showed up at the prayer meeting before dinner, she would tip her hand and the bishop would be on his guard. As a matter of fact, if she showed up at the dinner, that too would reveal her plan.

So, she had to find a way to intercept them when they slipped away this evening. She knew she might prevent them from sleeping together, but she also knew it might only *delay* it and cause her to lose a friend. She had to catch them and confront them after assuming it would surely happen. After all, the bishop's reputation as a ladies' man had preceded him, and if he didn't plan to sleep with Des, Lila would be extremely surprised.

A plan had developed in Lila's mind that evening. As the prayer meeting got underway in one of the hotel's conference rooms, she approached the front desk.

She smiled at the young clerk and said, "Hi, my name is Lila. I'm with the True Faith Christian group and I arrived early. But I found that the group has a block of rooms on the second floor. I'd like to check into my room."

The young man checked his computer and said, "I'm sorry, ma'am, but I don't see your name on the church group list."

"Well, I booked late and traveled on my own here. Could you please accommodate me? I work for Bishop Hines, and I'd like to room with my friend Desiree Carlson."

"I see, ma'am. Let me check with my supervisor."

After a head-to-head conference with an older woman, he returned to the desk. He said, "The hotel would be happy to accommodate you. I'll change your room and give you a pass card for room two ten." After checking her ID, the desk clerk did as promised.

Now Lila only needed to make herself scarce until it was time to spring her trap.

Wearing dark sunglasses, she decided to leave the hotel to lessen any chance of running into anybody from the group and exposing her plan. She made her way to the parking lot, got into her car, and headed out.

With nearly three hours to kill until dinner, Lila decided to get something quick to eat. Since she'd had nothing but coffee since morning, she found that she was hungry but not for a big meal. She did a little window-shopping after she ate, until it was time to go back to the hotel and enact her devious, yet well-meaning plan.

She hadn't been able to find out the bishop's room number since the hotel said that would violate its guest privacy rule. Besides, she already had pushed her luck with finding out Des's room number. She didn't want to cause any suspicions with the hotel.

Would they go to her room—or his? Without any experience in

surreptitious love affairs, she had to revert to her own logic. What would be riskier for them? Would it be far worse for someone to see him coming out of her room or her coming out of his? Was there any difference?

She concluded that there would be no way to tell. She could hang out in her room, which she was now sharing with Des, and catch them that way. But if they went to his room, she would miss her chance altogether.

She found herself lurking behind a potted palm, trying to be inconspicuous to passersby while deciding what to do and how to do it. She knew she had to keep the bishop and Desiree in sight if she was to have any chance.

When the dinner was over, the parishioners started to leave in small groups. Many of the people were older folks and would no doubt be tired and return to their rooms. Others went to the beach, and still others headed for the hotel's pool. She had to remain out of sight. So, like some movie spy, she settled herself in a comfortable lobby chair and hid behind a newspaper. She felt a little silly but didn't know what else to do. This spying game was tiresome. She had to keep peeking out from the paper without looking obvious.

When she thought it was safe, she headed for the first of several hotel bars with her adrenaline running high. She had trouble identifying anybody in the dim light. At the first bar, it took some time to determine that neither of her targets was there.

*Darn*, she thought. *I could have already missed them if they headed for the room. Then again, maybe I just need to keep on spying a little longer.* It seemed better than no plan at all. However, before she went upstairs, she would check out another bar.

Bingo! She spotted them sitting in a secluded booth. It was dimly lit, but clear enough for their after-dinner drink to appear innocent.

Lila couldn't just stand outside and keep peeking in. That would arouse suspicion. Did she dare go in? She eventually decided it was the only thing to do.

She planted herself in a seat at the end of the bar, farthest away from them and closest to the door. She ordered a nonalcoholic drink and paid for it immediately, knowing that she would be making a quick exit. She just hoped that nobody else from the group would wander in and see her. Church people usually avoided bars, but there was no guarantee.

She could wear her sunglasses, but it seemed foolish in the bar's muted light. However, she decided it would be the better part of discretion, so she slipped them on. When the young bartender noticed her, she said to him, "Eye condition. I have to wear them."

He simply nodded as if this explained the odd behavior.

Keeping her eyes on them without looking suspicious and being ready to leave quickly if they got up was harder work than she had thought. . She couldn't nurse the drink forever, so she found herself ordering a club soda to keep her spot at the bar legitimate.

Finally, about ten thirty, they got up. She now was forced to make a decision, which so far had eluded her. If she followed them, she couldn't ride the elevator with them. If she took the next car up, they would already be in one of their rooms. However, if she went up to the second floor before them and popped into her room, they still might be headed for his room. And she didn't know if that was on the second floor too.

She also didn't want to make the confrontation too soon, because it might not be obvious what they were planning to do. The only thing she was sure of was that they were planning to sleep together that night.

She made up her mind and dashed out to the elevators. When she got there, she changed her mind. It would be safer and quicker to use the stairwell, so she dashed up the stairs and planted herself in the hall near the elevator. She would catch them as they came off the elevator and go into her already planned act of a last-minute decision to make the seminar.

What could they do then? Continue on to one of their rooms together? Of course not!

She began fishing in her purse as she watched the elevator dial move up. When the first car stopped, she got ready. But they weren't on it. *Darn! Did they decide to go for a walk on the beach? Maybe go to another bar? Darn! Darn!*

She decided to wait for the next elevator car, but still had no luck. She was about to go to her room and call her plan a failure when they appeared on the next elevator car. She went into her purse-fishing routine and looked up when the two were almost upon her. When she first saw them, he had his arm around her shoulder. By the time they reached her, she sensed more before seeing his arm go down. She looked up and in a loud, surprised voice said, "Des. Hi. It's me. I decided to come after all!"

Des couldn't hide her surprise. Her eyes remained wide, her jaw slack, as she searched for words. "Oh…Lila…uh…hi. I—uh, we were just coming in from dinner."

Bishop Hines, the consummate actor, said, "It's so good to see you, Lila. I'm so glad you could make it. We were just saying how much we would miss you this weekend."

"Well, here I am," she said in her most jolly voice, doing a pretty good acting job herself. "I booked myself into your room."

Des said, "Oh, yeah, of course."

The bishop, not missing a beat, pulled out his room card, glanced at it, and said, "Let's see, they have me in room two fifteen. That's just down the hall. Well, ladies," he added, "I will bid you a good evening. And I will see you bright and early at breakfast."

Des, still looking stunned, said, "Ah, yes, Bishop. See you in the morning."

Lila said, "Good evening, Bishop. See you at breakfast." The girls headed for their room, with the atmosphere so palpable that Lila could feel it stirring up the plethora of emotions she was fighting.

# CHAPTER SIXTEEN

Lila claimed she was tired and went right to bed, and Des didn't have anything to say either. In the morning, Des still didn't have much to say, and she seemed unusually quiet. Lila wondered if she should bring it up. Or did Des get it? Maybe she knew what Lila was doing. Maybe she realized. In any case, Lila took the easy way out and held off all drama for now.

At breakfast, they were just having their first cup of coffee when Lamont—all smiles—approached their table. Now Lila was the one caught off her guard. While it shouldn't have been, it was a shock to see him.

"Good morning, ladies," he said cheerfully. "Could I join you?"

Lila just motioned, and Desiree seemed distant and said nothing. Lamont said to Lila, "I didn't think you were coming to this."

"I wasn't, but I had a last-minute change in plans and decided to come up on my own."

Lamont had a shopping bag, which he had set on the floor. "Look," he said, as excited as a kid. "Look what I got for the kids." First, he took out three blue T-shirts emblazoned with "Hilton Head, South Carolina."

"Looks like you got the right sizes," Lila said. She knew that most men wouldn't get that right. Still eagerly fishing in the shopping bag, he said, "Look at this for Latoya." He then held up a beautiful gold cross on a delicate chain.

Lila smiled. "She'll love that."

Next, he took out a video game, something to do with blasting space aliens, and held it up. "For Jackson," he said. "And last but not least, for the baby." He held up a toy boat with "Hilton Head" inscribed on it. "For the baths that he fights so much. Do you think they'll like these?"

Lila was touched. He was as earnest as a child—just as he used to be before their lives had been torn apart.

During breakfast, Lamont and Lila did most of the talking, with Lamont in the lead by far.

By Sunday morning, with the group assembled in the lobby and waiting for the coach, Lila and Desiree hadn't said more to each other than any other casual acquaintance. However, without saying it, both knew that something had happened.

Lamont came over to Lila as she was talking to some people. He said, "Hey, Lila. Could I ride with you?"

She had no reason to refuse. She agreed, although she was apprehensive. Why? She couldn't be sure. It was just that the weekend had been so stressful and full of emotions of every kind. As Lamont was throwing his bag in the backseat, she wondered why Des didn't ask to ride with her too.

She knew that this new, refreshing Lamont should have been no real concern to her for the few hours they would be together, but she was still tense. By the time they pulled into town, she was mildly surprised that he had breached no major issues. He had asked for nothing, promised nothing, and acted more like a dear old friend.

However, Lamont did have one request. "Can you drop me at the house? After I give these things to the kids, I can walk home."

"Are you sure? I can drive you."

"Nah. I like walking these days. It's like a whole new thing for me."

"How so?"

"You have no idea how refreshing it feels to be able to walk after you've spent so much time in a daze and not walking anywhere. It's like waking up from a bad dream and being so glad to realize that it was only a dream. I'm probably not relating it right, but believe me, you can't know what a thrill it is to take a simple long walk. And feel strong doing it."

She gazed at him thoughtfully, trying not to make much eye contact but still doing so. "I guess I don't know."

Before she could change direction, she was pulling into her driveway behind Bill's car because she wasn't even thinking about it. *Oh, God*, she thought. *Here come the fireworks.*

Thankfully, there weren't any. When Bill saw them arrive together, he was playing with Jackson. He eyed them coldly and then left with a mumbled good-bye. She could just guess what she was in for when she saw him at work.

The kids were ecstatic—but not only because of the gifts. They enjoyed the feeling of their parents being together and operating like a family again. At least for the short time Lamont was with them, it felt that way.

When she was alone, Lila tried to sort things out in her mind. Had she accomplished what she set out to do with Des and the bishop? She thought she had. Without a confrontation, she was sure Des would forge ahead with the affair. She thought she would confront her at Hilton Head and let the chips fall where they may. However, after all the tension, that task seemed too distasteful, and she just didn't do it.

*Did I think that as soon as I caught them, it would all go away?* She wondered. *Face it, girl; you didn't finish the toughest part of the job.*

On Monday morning at work, Bill was, as she expected, cold as ice. She confronted him immediately.

"Look," she said. "I went to the seminar for a different reason than what you're thinking. Not for Lamont. I didn't even think about him being there. He bought some things for the kids and asked if he could ride with me to the house. That's all that happened!"

Since he simply nodded and didn't ask her real purpose, she didn't bother to go into what she was thinking and feeling about Desiree.

Television crews suddenly appeared at the church to start the preliminary work for the bishop's new show. Their arrival proved a more substantial effort than making the documentary, for it took everybody's attention away from the immediate problems. Evidently, they weren't going to do it as many other TV evangelists did, though. Instead of some professional soundstage in the city, they were going to film everything right there at True Faith Christian.

People were overjoyed and couldn't keep away. They found any excuse to come down to the church to see what was going on. Many of them wound up in the bookstore, if only to browse and have an excuse to be around the excitement in the building.

So, with all the people in the bookstore, they were busier than ever. If not necessarily selling books, they were fielding questions and supporting all the reasons people had for being there. There was no doubt that the parishioners were as much into the 'Church of What's Happening Now' as the bishop was.

Lila commented to her salesclerk, "It's almost like they, too, feel they are special and part of the scene."

The girl said, "Well, aren't they? Aren't we all?"

Lila had to think about the simple wisdom of the statement. "Yeah, I guess we are. It isn't just about the bishop. It's about all of us."

As soon as she was alone with Bill, she knew she had a hassle coming. However, she wasn't about to leap in and start explaining. She let him make the first move.

His first comment was a bit apologetic, yet tinged with petulance. "You can't blame me for thinking what I immediately thought."

She leveled a steady gaze at him and made sure he didn't break eye contact. "Yes, actually, I can and do expect that you would understand and not think the worst of me."

"C'mon, Lila, I'm no superman. I can't help thinking what

anybody else would think. You lie to me about where you were going. You disappear for the weekend and show up with him."

"True enough. And maybe you had some reason for what you thought. *But,*" she said, emphasizing the word, "I thought we had a strong relationship that would go beyond petty jealousy. You want me to forget that we shared a life together and that he is the father of my children. I can't do that. Issues that will come up as they grow up will necessarily involve him. I know you wonder if I am harboring any feelings for him. I'm afraid, as far as that is concerned, that you'll have to believe what I tell you. After all, don't I believe you when you tell me how it is with you and your ex-wife?"

She paused. "Do you remember when we talked about the nature of jealousy? You and I—at least I thought—agreed that jealousy was more about being insecure than it was about loving someone."

He nodded.

"Well," she said, "I believe that. It seems you don't."

He remained silent, and the conversation ended there. Actually, there was so much going on around them with the TV people that a more serious discussion was impossible. There was always a technician searching for some kind of electrical connection, the caterer wondering where to set up, or the sound people trying to work in what was supposed to be an office atmosphere. When the sheer volume of curious onlookers was added to all this, the result was nothing but semi-organized chaos.

When the first program was aired, there was little doubt that Bishop Hines was about to become a major evangelical star. His rhetoric—a brand that was as fiery as it was compassionate—seemed to strike the right tone. Whenever his message appeared to be damning the sinners, it just as quickly lifted them up as one of God's most beloved and opened the door for redemption. It was different enough to set him apart from the gaggle of other evangelists who preached the same fiery brand of religion.

As a result, the bishop spent less and less time at True Faith Christian, leaving others, like Bill, to preach the sermons.

Lila happened to run into Desiree at a lunch spot, and if Lila didn't know better, she might have thought that her girlfriend was trying to avoid her. In any case, Lila greeted her with a cheerful, "Hey, girlfriend, where you been?"

"Oh, hi, Lila. I've been around." Desiree was almost forced to sit down and have lunch with Lila after that.

When they were settled, conversation between them didn't seem to flow as easily as usual. "What's the matter, babe?" Lila asked.

"Nothing. Nothing at all."

After a few more minutes of silence, Desiree spoke up. "You think I'm doin' the bishop right? Well, don't you?"

Lila stirred her coffee. "Yeah, I do."

"And you think that's a terrible thing."

"You're single, Des. He isn't. You shouldn't be messing with a married man." She forced a grin. "I say that because I love you. Not because I'm passing judgment."

"And that's why you came up to Hilton Head, right? To bust us up. Admit it."

"Yes. But I have a feeling that I'm whistling in the wind."

Desiree locked eyes with her. "Go ahead and tell me the truth, girl. Isn't it really because you think that the bishop is too good for the likes of me?"

Lila took her hand across the table. "If anything, I'd say just the opposite. You're too good for the likes of him, Des. He brings you close to accepting Jesus as your savior while seducing you with his words—and flesh."

Desiree looked torn. There was anguish in her features—the kind of anguish that Lila had never seen before. Speaking low, she said, "He is telling me how I can get my child up here from Alabama. I could be a mom, and I could have a life."

"Does he include himself in this scenario?"

"Well, not yet. But I feel he will, eventually."

"Why do you think that?"

Desiree's face softened. She said, "Lila, it's hard to explain. This here ole girl, as you know, been around. But, Lila, I tell you nothing—absolutely nothing—has ever been like this."

Lila squeezed her hand. "That's because you've never really been in love before. Oh, sure, you've been in lust many times, but never genuinely, deeply in love. And I think that with this man, you are."

"Oh, Lila." She was near swooning now. "It's something I…I never felt before. It's…so…" She couldn't finish.

"That's why I think it's so wrong. He's not going to reciprocate your feelings. He's doing what he's always done: taking his pleasure where and when he can. Now I'm convinced of it. He's one of those men who just loves women and loves to keep score."

Desiree listened intently, clearly chewing over her friend's words, and then said, "You sound like me, always warning you about men like Lamont. Users."

"Lamont's not a user, Des. He's someone who got off the right track. It's different."

Des said nothing.

"The men you are talking about are, of course, usually after one thing. But what's worse with the bishop is that he is messing with your faith and with your heart. Just think. You are on the verge of a huge breakthrough in your life. Just when you decide to give yourself to Jesus, he is tempting you with his flesh. That makes him the absolute worst kind of man."

"You probably right, Lila. But I just can't help the way I feel about him. I just can't help it. It's like it's beyond me. Like I ain't got no control of it. My heart and soul reacting without my consent. I know what you're saying is true. I just can't help it."

Lila listened intensely as Des poured her heart out about how special the bishop was to her. She went on this long monologue o f how gorgeous he was, how he uplifted her spirits and put Jesus in her heart and made life worth living. While she did understand Lila's point and inherently knew that sleeping with a married man was immoral, she couldn't shake the bonds that chained her to this charismatic man.

Was it because she had never met anyone like him? Or was it because nobody like him had ever taken such an interest in her? The latter part was the most flattering—that a man actually cared about her beyond what she could do for him in bed.

"Des, you've come a long way. You believe in Jesus now, right?"

“Oh, yes.”

“Is it because you’ve made the decision, or because you think that the bishop told you to and you don’t want to disappoint him?”

She had to think about that one. “Yeah, the bishop led me to Christ, but it’s me, Desiree, who loves Christ.”

Lila smiled. “Praise the Lord.” She lifted up her hands.

Des seemed confused. “Say what? You trippin’, girl?”

“No, I’m not tripping. I say, again, praise God. Praise him because you believe in him from somewhere in your own self, and you’re not completely driven by your love for the good Bishop Hines.”

“You serious. Aren’t you?”

“Darn straight, Des. Promise me something?”

“I’ll try. Promises are sometimes hard to keep.”

“Promise me that in whatever comes in your life—whatever is down the road—you will pray and rely on Jesus to help you. Don’t be waylaid by any man. Always believe in Jesus. Can you promise me that?”

Des thought for a while. “I hope so, Lila. I really hope so.”

She looked distant for a moment. “Man, life has become so hard. I only used to worry about where my next good time was coming from. Now, I gotta worry about true love and bein’ good for Jesus. I don’t know, Lila. I just don’t know. That man has me looking forward to tomorrow. I don’t know if I can just let him go like that. I just don’t know.”

Lila smiled. “Amen, sister. Join the rest of us.”

# CHAPTER SEVENTEEN

Lila knew her words had a powerful impact on Des, at least to a degree. However, Des still wanted the bishop. To spare Des's feelings, she wished she was wrong about him. She knew that she was the only true and genuine friend Des had and felt it was her duty to tell her friend the truth. Lila prayed that Desiree would accept the truth and not retaliate out of anger.

Lila convinced Desiree that she should test Bishop Hines's sincerity. Desiree feared she was no intellectual match for the bishop and was fairly convinced of it. Or was she? She pondered it more lately than she had ever thought about practically anything. Why? Because this man could awesomely satisfy her physical needs and her spiritual needs too. Not that she had ever dealt with such a man before…but how would she find out if he was cheating on her?

Of course, the bishop was married, so he was the one who was cheating. He gave her many hints that he was unhappy in his married life, too. Her name was Sheryl, and he complained that she was too uptight. He said she was far too inhibited for him, and that's what he loved about Desiree—she was totally unrestrained and passionate when it came to sex.

Her twisted sense of conceit thrilled her to think she was with a man who wanted her more than his own wife. She had never met Sheryl, but from what the bishop told her, she was more of the intellectual type and not the soulful, raw, man-pleaser he wanted. Did that mean he would leave Sheryl for her? And how could she replace a tailor-made preacher's wife even if he did? Sheryl was educated, articulate, and elegant—qualities much unlike herself.

But could she learn to be? These thoughts were driving her so crazy that often she wished she could revert to her old self.

What was different about her relationship with the bishop was that she didn't do anything in particular to please him. She was just herself. Apparently, that was vastly different from his wife, but whom was she fooling? She knew men, most men liked variety and welcomed a stranger when they could. Or was she limiting her knowledge of men to those she'd known? After all, she only knew she tended to meet the playboy types of men and rarely a man of quality or substance. Her boyfriends were barely this side of the law—if not on the other side.

*Shoot*, she whined to herself. *I'm a simple girl. I just want me a man who makes me feel like the bishop makes me feel. Why does life have to have so much damn drama?*

She was paying the bishop an impromptu visit to his office, which had been pressed into service temporarily as a dressing room. As she approached, Sheri, the secretary, casually tried to dismiss that she was there to see Bishop Hines.

"He's in makeup and can't be disturbed." Her attitude was curt and condescending and Des didn't appreciate it. *Welcome to the woman on the side.*

Des grinned. "Makeup? My, haven't we gone showbiz."

"You can't go in," Sheri insisted.

Des sauntered right past her and opened the door. The bishop was sitting back in a makeup chair, a towel over his eyes. The makeup girl, a saucy young thing with a blonde mane cascading down her shoulders, put her fingers to her lips, signaling silence.

Des motioned her over. At first, the blonde made a gesture that indicated she should leave, but something in Des's eyes must have encouraged her to join her.

"What?" she whispered as she approached. "He sometimes naps when I'm doing his makeup. You can't disturb him."

Des wrapped her hand around the girl's wrist. "Look, Missy, we're good friends. I got to see him. Now go away and come back later. Got it?"

The girl hesitated, and Des twisted her wrist and watched her pretty face contort in pain.

"Okay, okay, lady. Don't say I didn't warn you!"

With that, she tiptoed out, and Des locked the door and approached the dozing bishop. She stood for a moment, admiring his handsome face below the towel as he breathed softly. She knew how he liked to grab catnaps. She leaned over his face and pursed her lips, pressing them to his as her hand snaked down his belly. When it got lower, he squirmed a bit. Des pressed her lips harder to his, but he did not kiss her.

"What the…?"

When he flipped the towel off his eyes, he stared into the

grinning face of Desiree. “You little minx. What were you trying to do? Don’t you know we are on a movie set?”

“Don’t matter what I was trying to do. What matters is what you didn’t do.”

“What didn’t I do?” he asked, seeming puzzled.

“You didn’t lay back and let sweet Desiree make you feel like a man.”

The bishop’s face gleamed with delight. He said, “We can’t do anything here. What if…?”

“I locked the door.”

“But—”

Her kiss stifled his protest, and her tongue sought his. Soon they were in a world of their own.

On her way out, she stopped by the bookstore. Lila greeted her by saying, “Hi, babe, you made a special trip to see me?”

“Don’t be a wiseass there, girl. Of course, I come to see you. You got time to do lunch?”

“Sure.” And they were off.

Lila could tell that her friend was in an upbeat mood and that could only mean one thing these days. As they settled into a booth at the local lunch place, Lila turned to her. “Need I ask why you are in such a fine mood today?”

“Because you know I got my ways with men.”

“Oh, I know that.”

“No, smart-ass. I mean that I know how to put a man to the test.”

“What test is that?”

Lila knew Des wasn’t enthusiastic about telling her, so she calmly began eating her lunch and waited. Lila wiped the corner of her mouth with a napkin and said, “You should have checked your lipstick. You’re smudged.”

“Say what?” Des said, whipping out a compact and repairing the almost unnoticeable smudge. “What’s that makeup girl’s name?”

Lila grinned. “What? Did you have a run in with her?”

“Never mind. What’s her name?”

“I think I heard them call her Honey.”

“Honey, huh? She thinks she got some special privilege over

the bishop, 'tellin people who he can see and when! She ain't me."

"It's showbiz, Des. They're a different breed. Why? What happened?"

"I just wanted to see the man, and she acted like she was his guard."

"What did he say?"

"She said he was dozin' while she was putting on his makeup."

"So tell me what happened."

"I'll probably get in trouble, but I convinced her that I should see him if I wanted."

Lila took a sip of coffee and said with a smile, "Come on, Des, something happened that you want to crow about. That's what this is all about."

Des clearly couldn't hide the grin any longer. She said, "I done went in. He had a towel over his eyes. I put my lips on his."

"And?"

"And he didn't kiss me back. He threw off the towel, all ticked off."

"And so?"

"And so? Girl, in the circles I run in, if a strange woman comes in and plants one on a man, he gonna go for it."

"And you're tickled that he didn't. My gosh, how easily you are satisfied."

"May seem like a small thing to you, but I know men, and this one is different."

Lila didn't try to dampen her friend's mood. After all, if it made her happy, then she was fine with that. Although what she described was too trivial of a test.

Lila asked, "Tell me, has the bishop set up a date for your altar call? I've been thinking about it. Are you even ready?"

Des turned serious. "Yes, I am. Like I've never been more ready for anything in my whole life. But to answer your question—no, he's been so busy with this movie star stuff that he hasn't had time."

"But it will be soon, right?"

"I hope so. I've been looking forward to it. You know me. Sometimes I get so wrapped up in other things. But, no, nothing is more important to me." She gazed at Lila. "You happy for me?"

"Very."

"Girl, soon I may be getting everything I want in life."

"I hope so, Des."

"It's a scary thing to think about, ain't it?"

"It sure is."

After lunch, Lila took it upon herself to drop by the set to see for herself how things were going. The door to the office was ajar, so Lila peeked in and saw that Honey had just put the towel back on the bishop's eyes. She leaned over him and caressed his cheek with her lips.

He sighed and said, "Your perfume is so different. I've never encountered it before. It's so exotic."

"A friend sends it to me special from Egypt. It's unique—called Cleopatra's Sin."

"It is unique. Smells like nothing else. Cleopatra's Sin, huh?"

"Yeah, wanna try some?"

Her blonde mane fell over his face as her lips sought his and immediately Lila cleared her throat. Honey jerked suddenly away from the bishop.

"Oh, I didn't know you were standing there," said Honey.

The bishop removed the towel from his face and looked at Lila with surprise. "Well, it's good to see you, Lila. How are things going for you these days?"

"I am great in the Lord. What about you?" she asked, with cynicism.

"I'm well," he responded, with a nervous tone. "What do I owe this visit to?"

Before Lila could answer, Honey blurted out rudely, "How did you get pass the receptionist? I told Sheri not to let anyone come near the door."

"She must be on her break."

Honey left the room in a hurry to see where Sheri could have gone.

"I didn't want anything in particular, Bishop. I just wanted to see how things were going with the taping of the TV show."

"It's going well; thank you for stopping by. And oh, yes. I've been meaning to tell you what a fine job you're doing in the book store. Hiring you has certainly paid off for both of us."

"Yes, sir, it has. Well, I must be going now."

All sorts of thoughts were meandering in Lila's head as she headed for the door. *Was she really going to kiss him? What if I didn't interrupt?*

He started to say something, but she murmured, "The door's locked. Not to worry. Now you just relax. Honey is here."

# CHAPTER EIGHTEEN

When the call came that Lila's dad was ill, she packed up the kids in the car, threw their luggage in the trunk, and set out for the country. He was diagnosed with a form of cancer that required long-term treatment.

She told Bill that she would have to take a leave of absence from her job. She was going to have to rely on Lamont's payments to keep them going, which didn't exactly put her mind at ease.

It was hard to get into the kids' heads that they had to be quiet around Grandpa because he was sick. She hoped they would spend most of their time outdoors.

After three or four days, he was feeling a little better, and the first thing he wanted was a visit from the kids. "Hi, Grandpa," they all chorused. "Are you all better now?"

He smiled weakly and grasped each one by the hand. The kids were full of stories. "We were playing in the woods out back," one began. "Mommy showed us where she and Auntie used to play when they were kids like us."

Lamont called constantly, but her father didn't mind talking to him every day if he liked.

About a week later, Dad was feeling well enough to sit out in the porch in the sunshine, and Lila delighted in his progress. One afternoon they were drinking iced tea out on the porch. "Have you noticed how well Lamont's doing, he asked?"

"Sure I have, Dad, but you know we've seen this before. I have to be careful about getting my hopes up about him."

"You've got to admit that he's never been sober and gainfully employed since he left a couple of years ago."

"That's true, but I've been to all the drug clinics, and I know how bad the odds are of kicking drugs."

The old man sighed. "Now, Lila, you know that the Lord will do everything he can to help the boy. You should always have an optimistic attitude."

"I know, Dad. I guess I just need to protect myself from more heartbreak."

"I can understand that, my dear, but you've got to be upbeat. I've taught you that."

"So what magic did you do with Lamont?"

"No magic—just understanding."

The comment needed clarification, so she waited. She knew her dad, and she knew it was coming.

"You know that Lamont grew up without a father."

"Of course I know, Dad. He told me often that he felt like he'd missed a lot."

"He never had a male role model, so he picked up on the street what he thought a male should be."

"Yeah, but that's no reason to start using drugs, Dad. I hope that's not what you're telling me."

"No, not at all. All I'm trying to do is help you understand that his idea of being a man is to be a basketball star—and *that* he did. He also felt it was manly to be 'one of the boys' and do what everyone else was doing. So, when some of his friends started doing drugs, it seemed like a good way to numb the pain he suffered from."

"What pain?"

"The feeling of no longer being a hero—what else? The

feeling of being nobody again after he got that injury and couldn't play basketball anymore."

"And so he got hooked on drugs?"

"A mistake, true enough, but not a lapse in character. You know, he told me that when he was done being a basketball hero, he felt like less than a man. It affected his self-confidence that he couldn't still get the high praise he got from basketball. That lack of self-esteem led him to drugs."

Lila knew her dad was trying to get them back together, but she had her doubts about whether it could work out. She had lived with Lamont for years and didn't know the trauma he was suffering. Knowing Lamont, his effort to be manly in all things explained why he never discussed it with her. It was a real component that ultimately led to his downfall.

When a three-man delegation came to visit her father the next day, the old pastor looked terribly distressed. Lila asked, "What is it, Dad? What did those church elders tell you?"

"There's trouble with the new church. We got a construction loan, but there wasn't proper supervision and some of the work didn't pass building code inspection. It has to be done over. Sure, we can sue the old contractor, but that will take months—maybe years. In the meantime, we don't have a church. We have to raise more money, and we only have ten days to do it."

"Why only ten days?"

"That's when they'll inspect the progress on the construction again. If it's in compliance with the loan agreement, we'll get the money to finish then. If not, we're in default and can lose what we already have in."

Lila hated to see him so worried. She knew the stress could slow down, if not hinder, his recovery.

The next day brought a big surprise. It was Lamont. The kids swarmed all over him as usual and it warmed her heart to see it. However, Lila wanted to stay far away from him because she just couldn't bear any more disappointments.

When the old pastor explained the problem to Lamont, he seemed distressed.

After the kids were in bed and the old man was asleep, the estranged parents sat in the kitchen sipping coffee. It felt familiar and comfortable, and for the first time in two years, Lila wasn't worried that he might blow up or that something unpleasant would happen.

Evening shadows were falling, and they took their coffee out to the porch where they settled into rockers. A soft chilly breeze offered the invitation of an early fall before it whispered through the trees. A whip-poor-will in the nearby woods sang them an evening melody while a distant radio played country music with meaningful lyrics.

"Nothing like the country," Lamont said emphatically. "I don't care *what* city folk say."

"I know," she replied. "Sometimes I really miss it."

"I was down to the church construction site this afternoon."

"And?"

"It's a darn shame," he said. "All they need is a new footing, one that will go below the known frost line. That was one of the problems last time. They already poured the concrete, but it all has to be dug up if the foundation is going to be up to code."

"That's too bad. Dad has all his hopes in that church."

"As does the rest of the town."

The next afternoon, Lamont again went to the construction site. When he returned, Lila noticed a spring to his step as he approached her on the porch.

"I have an idea," he offered. "Do you think we can get a work force of, say, ten guys together?'

"I have no idea. Where would we get them from?"

"Doesn't your Dad still hold youth Bible study classes made up of young people? How old are those people?"

"Some are teenagers. The ones who take an interest in Bible study might be a little older, but why?"

"What do you say we get on the phone tonight and see if we can round up a ten-man crew? I think that with ten men, we might be able to get a new foundation in before the foreclosure date on the loan."

Lila tilted her head. "Do you think?"

"Yeah, I do."

When they put the plan before the old pastor, tears came to his eyes. "Go ahead, children. The Lord says we can do all things though Christ who strengthens us."

They got on the phone—Lamont on the house phone and Lila on her cell. Using her father's records, they contacted nearly forty people. Before the night was over, they had ten committed to being at the work site by eight the next morning. The old man was asleep when they finished, so they would wait until morning to tell him the good news.

Lila packed the kids in the car and went down to the building site at lunchtime. Women from the kitchen ministry fried loads of fresh fish left over from the church's fishing trip and served it with homemade potato salad to delight the crew.

While there were only seven young men at the site, it was encouraging. Lamont was covered with sweat from the late summer heat but smiled broadly.

"I'm pleased with the progress we made today. Look," he said, pointing. "We managed to get up about ten feet of the footing. I have to figure out yet where and how we're going to get more cement when it's all excavated, but that's for another day, babe." He then gave her a sweaty hug.

Lila grinned in response to it. "Yuck. I almost forgot what you farm boys smelled like."

"It's honest sweat," he confirmed. "We have to get on the phones tonight and see if we can get some more help."

That night, at dinner, Lamont was still enthusiastic as he explained the progress they had made through day's end. He knew some of his crew couldn't return, so he hoped they could get others to fill in.

"Hey, I met up with Jasper Collins," he said. "Remember him? He and I used to play hooky together and go fishing up at old man Johnson's pond."

"Yeah, I remember him. He was kind of a mama's boy—but a good-looking guy who just needed direction. I always thought he would make somebody a good husband. Is he married?"

"I don't think so. Why? You got somebody in mind?"

"Maybe," she replied with a smirk.

Lamont merely shook his head.

They seemed to have made progress by the time Lila showed up with lunch, but it was fleeting at best. Only five men had shown up, but she could see that Lamont still set about the task enthusiastically. “Without a backhoe, we have to dig this foundation out and lift it by hand,” Lamont explained. “That’s what’s taking so long.”

“Yeah. But we’ve only got—what?—eight days left.”

That night they led a prayer group at their house, asking the Lord to help them to build his house, and in the morning, they had a crew of eight men.

Lila knew in her heart that they would probably fall short, but it was wonderful to see everybody working together to do the Lord’s work. That day she got hold of the local Yellow Pages and began calling backhoe companies. She planned to ask for credit for backhoe work or the loan of a backhoe for the church basement excavation.

Lamont returned that night sweaty, dirt-covered, and exhausted, but Lila had good news for him. “I’ve got a backhoe!” she exclaimed.

“Say what?”

“I got a company to lend us a backhoe, as long as we have

someone qualified to operate it. They know Dad and said they would like to help."

"Supercool. I worked enough construction to know how to operate a backhoe. Tell them that and ask them where can we pick it up from."

"They said to just provide a qualified driver and they would deliver it on one of their flatbed trucks."

"Cool," Lamont said, clearly thrilled at her efforts and the positive response.

The next afternoon when Lila brought lunch, Lamont was busily excavating concrete from the old foundation.

"How's it going, she asked?"

"Great, babe; just great."

Munching on a sandwich she had made him, he gleefully gave her a progress report. "It's going to be close, but I think we can make it." Then, he added, "If we get at least five more guys."

That evening, Lila and her sister Sandi, who came over to help, called up every old school chum they could think of. "This reminds me of old times doing church work, like bake sales, school plays, and all that stuff," Lila said.

"Yeah," Sandi said, "the PKs doing the Lord's work together again."

The next day, with only three days left, they had twelve men at the work site, but there was still much work to do. They were able to get credit from the concrete company to pour the concrete and planned to do it on Monday, the last workday.

"How did you get credit?" Lamont asked.

"I appealed to their community spirit," she said, smiling. "Word got out about the volunteers working on the church foundation and they offered to give us the concrete on credit. We promised we'd pay it off with our first collections, and they agreed."

"Praise the Lord," Lamont said.

They double-checked the contract and found out that the loan was due on Monday. However, because Monday was a holiday, this gave them an extra day to get more work done. If they could get everybody to work on Monday, they might make it.

On Monday, they had a volunteer workforce of six men, and

using the backhoe, they were done by seven that night. It would be up to the city inspectors to give them the green light on the work they had done, and now all they could do was pray.

On Tuesday morning there was Lila, Sandi, Lamont, the kids, and several of the volunteers waiting on the inspectors. It was no surprise that when they came, there wasn't a finger in the group that wasn't crossed and a kneecap that wasn't worn.

When the inspection was over, the smiling inspector handed them a completion certificate, which the bank loan officer was pleased to accept. There was more work to do, but they had saved the church's project. The old pastor's face lit up at the news, and it suddenly seemed like years had been added to his life.

Later that evening, Lila and Lamont sat on the front porch after dinner and truly relaxed for the first time in two weeks.

Through the whole thing, Lila and Lamont had gotten along and worked well together. Along with the kids, they felt like a family again—as they used to be.

As they reminisced about the completed church project, Lamont suggested going out on the town to celebrate the next night. Lila was excited about going out with Lamont. It reminded her of old times as they ate dinner by candlelight at one of the new local restaurants. The couple basked in the glow of accomplishment and their newfound sense of togetherness.

Neither of them planned it, but after dinner, they went on a drive through the countryside, where they enjoyed the scenery and the fresh air. Lamont drove to a familiar place where they used to sneak off to when they were in high school. He parked the car and rolled down the windows before asking her sweetly, "Do you remember when we use to come here, Lila?"

"Yes, I remember each time."

When Lamont leaned over and kissed Lila, a flame ignited within her soul. They were in each other's arms, clutching so tightly that Lila could hardly breathe. Lila felt as if she were drowning in love, struggling against the tide of passion that threatened to consume them in its fire. It was glorious. A new beginning. A renaissance. A renewal of life and love.

When they finally separated, sweaty and panting for breath, it was obvious that they had no choice but to go on with their lives together. Lila felt serene bliss on the drive back to her dad's house. And there was no question that the earnest smile on Lamont's face signaled he felt the same.

In a few weeks' time, the old pastor was well enough to resume his duties, and so he went back to them. By a small miracle, the old pastor felt well enough to conduct services, which were temporarily being held in the town library. He gave thanks to the Lord and everyone who helped with the project and stressed the importance of faith.

# CHAPTER NINETEEN

Bill seemed to know it the minute he saw Lila's face. Taking her by the hand, he confirmed it. "You got back with Lamont."

She nodded her face sadly. "I'm sorry, Bill. It's better for both of us this way. You may not think so now, but with the Lord's help, you'll see that it is."

He concealed his pain by hugging her and walking away.

Lila was glad to have Lamont move back in with her and the kids. The old hometown had a positive effect on them beyond the miracle that took place there. A whole way of living, along with the feeling of doing work for God and His church, spoke to them. Together they had a wonderful feeling—one that neither had experienced in a long, long time.

Lamont approached her one day and said, "Would you think I was crazy if I suggested that we move back home and bring the kids up the way we were brought up?"

Lila smiled. "I didn't want to do any boat rocking, but I've been thinking the same thing." When he hugged her, it felt so right, so natural. It was a feeling of contentment that she hadn't felt in a long time.

Even as Lila thought about her new plans, she wondered about Des. She hadn't seen her in a while, and she'd thought for sure she'd show up as soon as she heard Lila was back. And she would have known if Des had been by the bookstore.

Lila went by her house, but she wasn't home. They told her at work that she'd quit her job several weeks ago, and Lila began to worry that she had left town.

Somehow, Lila caught up with her at the park. Going to the park was a new thing for Desiree. She went there to think, to pray, and to find peace—something Lila had encouraged her to do—by finding solitude to get in touch with the Lord.

Des was sitting on a bench, looking sad but calm when Lila approached. "Hey stranger, I've been looking for you."

Des looked up. She'd been deep in thought but got up and hugged her friend and began sobbing. "Hey, I wasn't gone that long," Lila said, trying to pep her up.

Des shook her head, and they both sat down. Dabbing at her eyes with a handkerchief, she said, "I never could stand women who blubbered over their men."

"What man are you talking about? Or do I already know?"

"You know."

"Want to tell me about it?"

"Before I do, tell me about you and Lamont. You guys get back together?"

Lila just nodded with her own Mona Lisa smile. "Yeah, and I can't tell you how wonderful it is. But now's not the time for that. What's going on? Tell me."

"You were right. He did me bad."

"What do you mean?"

"I caught the bastard myself. I got to thinkin'. Remember I told you that he was faithful to me by not kissing that makeup girl?"

"Yeah, you felt good about that."

"Yeah, well…"

"What happened?"

"See, the problem is that I'm not used to dealing with clever men like Mack Hines. I'm more used to the type that I outsmart any old day. So, the next time I went to the bishop, he was taping his show and Miss Honey was out in the reception area, and I noticed how different her perfume was. I asked her about it, and she told me it was some special scent she got from someplace in the world."

"So?"

"So, old Mack Hines couldn't help knowing the difference between that perfume and my old-fashioned Chanel. *He knew it was me and not her.*"

"Oh, Des, how could you be sure? I…"

"I went further, girl. I went to see him when he wasn't expecting me. In fact, I made sure to tell him I wouldn't be around for a few days—that I was gonna go to the country and visit with you."

Lila was sitting on the edge of the bench now, eagerly awaiting the rest of the story.

"So I went on over to the office at lunchtime," Des said.

"You caught him with her?"

Des shook her head. “No. I didn’t catch him with her.” She raised her voice a bit. “I caught him with Miss Sheri.”

“His secretary?”

“Yeah.”

“So what did you do? Wait a minute,” she said. “I know you. Did you burst in there and bop somebody?”

“No. I decided that ole Des would be cool. She wouldn’t go makin’ no scene. No, I had to do the right thing, and to do that I needed to stay cool.”

She dug in her huge pocketbook and pulled out a cell phone camera, flipped it open, and showed Lila the pictures. There were five and in living color. The pictures displayed Bishop Hines more than the woman, because the woman was straddling him with her back to the camera. The woman was obviously naked, and the look on Bishop’s face left no doubt as to what they were doing.

Lila’s hand went to her chest. “Wow! That’s terrible.”

Des was calm. “Yeah, it sure is. When you think of how many people—people we know—look up to him and put their spiritual lives in his hands…these people believe in him more than they believe in anyone else. And now he's reaching people all over the country with his TV show."

Lila took Desiree's hand. "Des, because men, even men of the church, can be weak, we don't need to link the messenger up with the message. What he preaches is still true, even though he's not living up to it himself."

"I think I done figured that out. I know that the Lord wants us to do what Mack Hines tells us but not what Mack Hines himself does."

"Des, the Lord wants you to put all your trust and faith in Him, and He is one who will never let you down."

The two friends sat quietly on the park bench for a while. They listened to the birds chirping and watched as stray squirrels dashed around gathering nuts for the coming winter.

Eventually Des said, "See those squirrels? God's dumb creatures, right? But even they got enough sense to know that they need to store up food in the summer for winter or they ain't gonna have anything to eat. Surely, the Lord made His people at least as smart as a squirrel. So I asked myself what I should do. Should I expose him, make a fool out of him, and make myself feel good?"

"Sounds like a good idea to me," Lila said.

"Yeah, I could do that. But what would be best for the most people? Remember, we have to think about what the Lord said about His people."

Lila quoted the verse: "What you do for the least of these my brethren you do for me."

"Right, so I asked myself what would do the most good. And just before you got here, I think I figured it out."

Lila remained silent. Then she said, "Are you going to tell me?"

"I'm going to go see Mack Hines right now. Notice I don't dignify him with the title of bishop?"

"Yeah, I noticed."

"I'm going to go see him and tell him what's gonna be."

Des got up and walked to her car with a determined look on her face. She called over her shoulder, "When I've done it, I'll call you."

Des proceeded to True Faith Christian Church and walked into the bishop's office. Sheri tried to stop her at the door, but Des blew right past and entered bishop's office. He was sitting behind his desk.

"Hello there, beautiful. How are you with the Lord this fine day?"

"I'm good with the Lord, Mack. Question is: how are you?"

He was clearly startled by her manner and the use of his first name. He composed himself, however, saying, "What brings you here, my dear?"

She pulled out her camera, pressed the button, and handed it to him. He did a double take before looking at it. When he did, his jaw dropped.

She said, "Keep pressing the button; there's a whole bunch. Of course, it's only with one woman. I didn't have time to get all the rest."

He slumped back in his chair. "Sweetie, what are you gonna do with these?" he asked as he clutched the camera.

She grinned. "Don't worry; I got a lot more copies of those."

"But what…what are you going to do?"

"I'm gonna let the world know what a snake you are."

"But why? What will that solve?" His voice was beginning to sound a bit panicky. "Look at all the people you'll be disappointing."

"Oh, so you've thought about that too. You know all the people that you'll be disappointing I'm sure."

"Of course. I know I'm a weak man. But that doesn't diminish my ministry. It doesn't change what I'm here for, nor the message I have for the faithful."

She sat down in a nearby chair. "Ya know, I cringe to hear you use the word 'faithful.' You're not faithful to anybody—not yourself, your wife, your congregation, the Lord, or anybody."

The bishop looked thoughtful. "That's not true. You only know the superficial me. I don't let anybody know what's inside me."

She smirked. "I know what's inside you."

He grew solemn before saying. "If only God had made me…well…"

"Well what? Ugly?"

"Well, yes. It is *so* hard with women coming on to me all the time."

"Oh, please! Bishop, don't make me laugh. Poor you. You're saying that you're so handsome that you can't help all these women wanting you?"

"Look, do you want money? I can give you money."

She grinned impishly, happy to be in the driver's seat. "You gotta understand other people, Bishop. I ain't never been in such a good position—a position where I call the shots."

"Oh, I do understand, Desiree. So, how much money do you want?"

She cocked her head and rocked her crossed leg. "Let me see now. I gotta think about this. Now, how much do I want?"

"Be reasonable, woman. I'm just starting to make the big bucks. Don't go robbing me."

"You mean like you been robbing the church?"

He became defensive and tried to convince Des that the church's money was being used for a great cause. Des put her hands on her hips and stared at him in appalling fashion.

When he saw her face darken with determination, he looked scared. He said, "Now don't go asking too much."

Des said, "Now, Bishop, you surely know that the Lord never gives us more of a burden than we can bear."

"So…how much?"

She uncrossed her legs, leaned forward in her seat, and made eye contact with him. "I don't want any of your dirty money 'cause that wouldn't make me any better than you, now would it? Here's what I want. I want you to give up this TV gig you got going."

He jumped up from his seat. "What? Why? Why should I?"

"Because I'll release these pictures to the media. That's why."

"You wouldn't!"

"Why not? Do you know me? Did you ever bother to get to know me? How do you know what kind of person I am? How do you know what I'll do?"

"Well, I just know you're a kind, loving woman, Desiree. Why would you want to go and destroy a man just because you're jealous?"

With utter disbelief, she said, "So that's what you think it's all about. I'm jealous? How about *you* telling *me* you loved me—that *Jesus* loves me."

"Well, all that's true. Just because I'm weak doesn't mean that's a lie."

"Boy," she muttered, shaking her head. "I see now how you're so successful. You actually *believe* you have different standards for yourself."

He stared at her blankly, his eyes vacant like a man who had gone into shock.

"No," she said firmly. "The only deal I'll accept is that you drop this gig."

Bishop Hines looked stricken.

"Cheer up, Mack. In a while, when I'm outta your hair, maybe you'll want to try again. Maybe you can convince the world that my pictures are just a lot of hogwash rigged up by a jealous woman. Trouble is, with all the people checking into your finances these days, right now might not be a good time to try to do that."

Hines seemed to be thinking seriously about what she said. He looked up at her with curiosity.

Des said, "You didn't know this ole country girl had enough brains to pull this off, did you? You're shocked. You're flabbergasted. You thought all the women who were after you were the same. Dumb. Too dumb to even have a thought except for you."

He sat looking like his world had collapsed.

Desiree got up. "Well, Mack, I'll be going. If I don't see your resignation on TV real soon, I'll do what I gotta do."

After gaining some composure, Bishop Hines stood up with anger. As he towered over Des, he said, "Let me warn you, Des; you won't get away with this. I am well loved by a lot of high-powered people, and when they hear of this, I can't be responsible for what they might do to you."

"My, my, my, you ain't nothing more than a street hoodlum in a suit—or should I refer to the word of the good book, which describes someone like you as a wolf in sheep's clothing? Yes, that's exactly what you are. Just cancel the show."

Federal agents stormed in as Desiree began walking away. They were flashing their badges and brandishing a warrant. One agent said, “Mack Hines, you are under arrest for fraud and embezzlement.” While reading him his Miranda rights, they handcuffed Bishop Hines as Desiree watched in amazement. For a brief moment, she felt sorry for the bishop, but just as soon as that feeling came, it went.

That afternoon, Desiree told Lila what she had done along with the spectacular arrest of Bishop Mack Hines that was soon to make the news.

Lila was amazed. “That’s terrific,” she told her friend. “See, you didn’t have to bring him down. He did it to himself. The good book says that whatever is done in the dark, God will bring it to the light.”

“Yeah, you’re right.”

“You could have been rich,” said Lila.

“You right about that too, girlfriend.”

“And still you did the right thing.”

“Right again.”

However, the smirk had left her face. She put her arm around Lila's shoulders and said, "Girl, if it wasn't for you, I wouldn't have done none of this. Oh, I still woulda' jumped Mack Hines's bones, you can believe that, but I'd have taken that money too!"

Lila said dubiously, "Desiree, it wasn't me who did it for you. It was you. Something in you—something that's always been in you, that made you confront him."

"Now I'm going back to Alabama to see what I can do about getting my child back," Desiree said. "Then I'll be back."

Tears welled in Lila's eyes. "You'll come back, won't you?"

"'Course I will, girl. I ain't got no other best girlfriend."

Lila let the tears flow as she watched Desiree walk away. She thought of the wonder of God to use people we'd never guess to accompany us on our spiritual journey in life—in love, in our families, in church and in friendship—and the fleeting wisdom we embrace when, by chance, we take the time to think about it.

# Epilogue

It was a cool fall morning. The leaves were turning rusty red and settled underfoot everywhere in the little Georgia town.

Lila, Lamont, and the kids were walking into the new church. They went to the front pew and took their places. It was dedication day, and Lila's father was up on the pulpit, telling the people how their new church managed to be built. He left nothing out but gave all the credit to Lamont, the volunteers, and his daughters, Lila and Sandi, who helped throughout.

The pastor looked out at the congregation with a serious loving expression and asked if anyone wanted to accept the Lord as his Savior. A hush fell over the church as Desiree, without hesitation, approached the altar, a look of joy on her face. A tear fell from Lila's eyes.

When the service was over, everyone was outside, shaking the pastor's hand and talking about the new church. Everyone was in love with the little white church with the elegant steeple. It stood as a monument of love for the entire community.

Desiree came up to Lila, Sandi, and their families. Lila said, “I want to make sure that you’re coming home with us for dinner.”

“I sure am,” she said, motioning to a tall young man standing nearby and smiling. “Especially when I heard that that handsome dude over there is coming to dinner too.”

Lila glanced over to where she motioned. Lila and Lamont exchanged a smile. Lila said, “You mean Jasper Collins?”

“That’s who I mean. That man is fine—and he loves the Lord.”

# Contact the Author

Sharon B. Burgess

P. O. Box 393092

Snellville GA 30039

Sharon Burgess

P.O. 393092

Snellville GA, 30039

Email: Sharon@unraveledfaith.com

Website: Sharonbburgess.com

CPSIA information can be obtained at www.ICGtesting.com
Printed in the USA
LVOW01s2309240715

447607LV00001B/1/P